NOTHING IN COMMON

A HE'S TOO HOT TO BE TRUE ROMANCE

MEGAN HART

Copyright © 2010 by Megan Hart

All rights reserved.

No part of this book may be reproduced in any form or by any electronic or mechanical means, including information storage and retrieval systems, without written permission from the author, except for the use of brief quotations in a book review.

ISBN: 978-1-940078-51-9

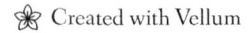

❀ Created with Vellum

AUTHOR'S NOTE

Nothing In Common was originally published in 2002.

DEDICATION

To Billy Zane for being just too darned pretty

CHAPTER 1

Men like that should be illegal.

The man standing across the room from Lila Lazin was utterly, unquestionably perfect. Broad, strong shoulders, flat stomach, narrow hips, long, lean legs. His midnight-colored hair was cropped short around his smooth neck and perfectly shaped ears, but left longer on top so the errant pieces fell across his forehead to brush eyes a pure light hazel, like amber touched with green, contrasting sharply with the brows the same inky shade as his hair. His strong, firm jaw and sensuous lips looked as though they could bring a woman to her knees with one kiss.

Some other woman, maybe. Handsome men were like bargain basement grab bags. They came in attractive packages that promised an exciting surprise inside, but once you got them home, all you ended up with was a bunch of junk. He'd spout words as pretty as his face until a better prospect came along, just like her last boyfriend had done. Though it had been over for two years, the memory still stung enough to make her rattle the ice cubes in her glass. William Darcy had told her he'd only dated her to do her a favor. He'd left her for a woman who looked like she'd been built from the Everyman's Dream catalog.

No, Lila had been there, done that, didn't need to do it again. Men who looked like that were great as eye-candy, but anything beyond that, she could do without. Unfortunately, he'd caught her staring. With a slight smile playing about his incredible mouth, he headed toward her. Now she'd done it.

It's all fun and games until someone catches your eye.

"Excuse me, but I couldn't help noticing you from across the room," the object of her attention said.

His voice, low but not rumbling, smooth like silk, went straight to the pit of her stomach, where it took a sharp turn south. Satin sheets and candlelight, she had time to think before he spoke again and saved her from her own long-ignored and petulant libido.

"Have we met before?"

That mouth and those eyes might be thigh-opening, but his opening line left her flatter than day-old beer. In a way, it was a relief. A convenient buffer against his unbelievable face and perfect body.

"I don't think so."

"I'm sure I've seen you before. I'm pretty good with faces," he insisted.

"Me, too, and I'm sure I would have remembered yours." Distracted by the sight of his mouth moving, she spoke before she knew it. Her cheeks heated as she realized what she'd said. Of all the idiotic replies! Not that he seemed to mind or even notice. Then again, a man who looked like he did must surely be used to women drooling and fawning all over him.

He smiled and stuck out his hand. "Tom Caine."

"Lila Lazin." She allowed him to capture her hand with his for a moment. His fingers were warm.

The silk of her dress began to rub her in all the right places. Lila shifted, and the cloth whispered first on her stocking-clad legs, then higher up, against the bare skin of her thighs. Damn her laziness for not buying more pantyhose. She'd thrown on a garter belt and stockings earlier because she had no pantyhose without runs, and they'd suddenly started to seduce her. She forced herself to stand still, even though the pressure of his fingers on hers still made her want to squirm.

"Lila." Tom mouthed her name as though tasting it. "I had a goldfish named Lila once."

He'd managed to tease a smile from her. "I was named after my great-grandmother. I don't believe she ever had a goldfish."

They stared in silence for a few minutes, until Tom gestured at the crowded room. "Quite the party."

Lila nodded. "It certainly is."

Her sister's paintings always drew large crowds. Rivka Delaney had won Best Local Artist in Capital Magazine's Best Of Central PA Contest over other, more prominent Pennsylvania artists for two years in a row. Tonight's theme centered around Rivka's latest project. Teasingly called "The X-Men" after a popular comic book series her husband adored, Rivka had done twenty portraits of local men: businessmen, doctors, accountants, cashiers at the local grocery store, the janitor from her building. Though they came from many different backgrounds, Rivka had somehow looked at each of them and found something—an expression, a way of standing—that made even the ones who were not "classically" handsome look like models. It was Rivka's gift. She had a way of finding whatever beauty the subject had inside and bringing it to the canvas.

"I love Rivka Delaney's work." Tom pointed at the piece directly behind them and sipped from his drink. "I have some of her prints at my house. I'd love to have an original, but they're hard to come by."

Lila watched the way his smooth throat worked with every swallow, and her own mouth went a little dry. Pretty face, she reminded herself sternly. Bargain basement junk.

"Rivka doesn't like letting go of her paintings."

"You know her?"

Lila glanced over her shoulder toward the knot of people surrounding her flamboyant sister. "I guess you could say I've followed her career since she started."

He gave her that stunning grin again. "Lots of people here tonight."

"Yes."

"You're a woman of few words, aren't you?"

It's because I want to use my mouth for other things than talking, Lila thought and gave herself a mental shake. This was dangerous ground. It had been a long time since a man had affected her this way, but she knew all too well the end results. She didn't answer, just gave him a raised eyebrow that made him laugh. He tipped his head back so she could see the smooth motion of his Adam's apple as it bobbed in his throat.

Oh, he's perfection. Absolute, sheer, unadulterated perfection.

"Listen." Tom leaned in closer to her. "Crowds drive me bonkers. How about we go someplace quiet and have a cup of coffee? We can talk about Rivka's work."

He'd done it again. The cheesy pick-up line, meant to melt her like butter. Lila supposed it worked on most women, him being the beautiful specimen of manhood that he was and all, but she wasn't most women. She breathed deep, grateful to have resisted his siren song.

"I don't drink coffee."

"Brrrr." The curve of his smile didn't affect her so much this time. "Did it just get colder in here or is it me?"

"Look." Lila attempted to soften her comment. "I'm sure you're not used to being turned down. It's just that—"

"What's that supposed to mean?" His full lips thinned as his smile vanished completely. "I'm not used to being turned down?"

Lila tilted her chin, knowing she'd put her foot in something, but not willing to admit what. "Men like you aren't used to having women tell them no."

"Men like me?"

Heat flared higher in her cheeks.

"I meant men who look like you." She paused and gestured toward the painting on the wall behind them. "X Men."

His hazel gaze flickered, unreadable. "Is that what you think?"

The heat in her cheeks deepened. "Haven't you ever looked in a mirror?"

"Haven't you?"

Lila gave a short, sharp laugh. "I know what I look like."

"So do I. You look like someone I'd like to get to know."

Her laugh was genuine this time, surprised out of her. "You should write a book. A thousand and one cheesy pick up lines."

"Come for coffee with me, and I'll give you a cut of the royalties."

He was pursuing her. Lila let her gaze slide over his perfect features, imagining those full lips on hers. A man like that would probably be too sure of himself in bed. Too certain he knew how to push her buttons. Too cocky, too arrogant...but oh, so easy on the eyes. And it had been a long, long time since she'd had any man's hands on her....

She stood straighter and made her voice more aloof. "I told you I don't drink coffee."

"Tea then."

Lila sighed. "Why are you doing this? Why me?"

"Why not you?"

Lila waved her hand at the crowd in the gallery. "This room is filled with models, actresses, and other biologically blessed females. Why not ask one of them? Why me?"

"None of those other biologically blessed women, as you call them, are standing in a corner looking interesting. They're all swarming around each other, trying to sound interesting...and failing."

She knew the lingo. Interesting meant the same as "she has a nice personality." William flashed in her mind again, and heat turned to ice. She wasn't interested in being any man's pity fuck. She turned to move away. "I don't think so."

Tom caught her elbow. An electric tingle went all the way up her arm, a sensation so fierce it made her actually stumble. He reached out with his other hand and kept her from falling, like something out of some corny romantic comedy.

Her breath caught in her throat. His hands, each large enough to wrap the fingers entirely around her upper arms, seared imprints on her bare skin. The scent of him, some cologne she couldn't name, tantalized her nostrils. The scrape of her garters on soft flesh too long neglected made her bite her lip, and she spoke before she could stop herself. "All right. Tea then."

Tom jumped up and punched the air. "Woo-hoo! She said yes!"

Embarrassed, Lila looked around to see if anyone had noticed his antics. As he had already pointed out, however, everyone in the room was competing with someone else to sound more profound, witty, or esoteric. Nobody was looking into the corner she shared with him.

"Don't." She had to laugh. "Do you do everything with this much enthusiasm?"

"Everything."

His answer sent another flash of heat through her. Lila could just imagine all the things Tom Caine did with enthusiasm. "Let me just get my coat."

"I'll get it for you. I've got to get mine, too."

She needed a few minutes to compose herself. "No, really, I can get it—"

Tom held up his hand to silence her. "Lila, I'm not trying to set back women's rights here or anything. I'd just like to get your coat for you. If it will make you feel better, you can get mine for me."

He had made her laugh again, which was actually more of an accomplishment than making her sigh. It seemed the pretty face had something of a sharp wit behind it. She handed him her claim ticket.

"It's a mustard-colored field coat with a plaid scarf."

She watched him wend his way through the crowd with far more grace than such a large man should have. He didn't stop to ogle the half-naked society belle who had staked herself out in front of one of Rivka's larger works, with champagne in hand and a gaggle of sycophants surrounding her. Though the woman clearly saw him, even angling her body to watch him pass, Tom didn't even look her way. Lila was impressed despite herself.

"What a tramp." Rivka's familiar husky voice sounded just beside Lila's ear.

"She seems to be enjoying the show," Lila noted dryly, returning her sister's hug.

Rivka waved one bangled arm. "So? She hasn't bought anything from me, and she sure could afford to. She's just here to get her picture in the paper, Lila-love. But how do you like the show?"

"It's wonderful, as usual." She did love her sister's art. It was bold and sassy, sometimes sexy or sentimental, just like her sister.

Rivka's skin-tight, black sheath dress dipped down to the dimples of her back and was covered by a sheer, flowing overdress of purple gauze. On her feet were thigh-high, red leather boots with heels tall enough to bring Rivka almost, but not quite, up to Lila's five feet, six inches. A multi-colored set of bangles on one arm was offset by the simplicity of a single gold chain around her neck.

Rivka saw her sister's look and shook her hips. "You like?"

"It looks like something Mick picked out."

"Are you kidding?" Rivka's hoarse, throaty laughter made both men and women turn their heads. "Mick wanted me to ditch the black dress and come in just the purple thing."

And she'd look great in that, too, Lila thought, just a trifle jealously. They both shared the same dark chocolate-colored hair and the same startling blue eyes. They even had the same thick, untamed brows. So why did it all come together on Rivka's face looking like a million bucks, while the face Lila saw in the mirror barely registered a dollar and change?

"Why didn't you?"

"That's not the way I wanted to get my face on the front page." Her sister pressed a lipsticked kiss to Lila's cheek. "Gotta run, Lila-love. I see Martin over there chatting up one of my best customers."

In a cloud of purple gauze, Rivka skipped her way through the crowd to meet with her agent. Lila watched her go, unable to keep from smiling. Her sister, the artiste.

"Ready to go?"

Lila turned to find Tom holding out her worn field coat as though it were some sort of offering. "Sure."

He settled the coat around her shoulders and lifted her hair free of the collar before smoothing the material flat on her shoulders. That simple, attentive gesture stunned her and made her throat close with sudden, inexplicable emotion. Clearing her throat and stepping away from his grasp, Lila forced a smile. "I'm ready."

"Me, too." His smile made her shiver, and Lila realized she'd lied. She wasn't ready for Tom Caine.

Not at all.

The tea had grown bitter in the pot, but Tom drank it anyway. Sitting across from Lila was a sweetness that more than made up for the brew's taste. They'd been sitting for three hours at MJ's Coffeehouse at the Allen Theater, discussing everything from college theater classes to practical jokes gone awry. She had a keen sense of the ridiculous that delighted him. On top of that, she was bright and not afraid to let him know it.

She's definitely not the sort of woman he was used to taking out, he thought, watching as she tucked a curl of coffee-brown hair behind one of her ears. Lila had long and slender fingers, nails short and neat, unadorned by any rings. Her face glowed with good humor, not makeup. Her features were slightly too uneven to be called beautiful, but her eyes were vivid blue ice and her mouth was damn near perfection. Her lips were full and soft, one front tooth slightly crooked enough to snag his tongue if he wasn't careful. He didn't plan on being careful. No, Lila Lazin wasn't like the hardbody hotties he normally went out with. She was smart and funny, and Tom was completely and utterly smitten.

"So anyway," she was saying, "I had just finished flushing the damn thing down the toilet when the phone rang. It was my roommate, asking about the fish!"

"Weird." Tom drank in the way Lila's smile curved her mouth.

"Candace was weird," Lila agreed and then broke off. She had noticed him looking at her mouth. "What?"

"Just thinking about how much I'd like to kiss you right now," Tom answered honestly.

Lila flushed and then frowned. She pulled her glance from his and began intently studying the mug of tea in her hands. Her face told him he shouldn't have blurted out his thoughts. It was a fault of his—that tendency to speak without thinking. He hadn't thought her reaction would be so negative. She'd made it clear from the start she wasn't impressed with lame conversation, but he wasn't trying to come on to her...at least not in a sleazy way.

"Lila, I'm sorry." He was apologizing for his bluntness, not his desire to kiss her. He couldn't be sorry for that.

"We were having a nice time." Her voice was quiet, and she still didn't meet his eyes.

"We still are." He felt stupider than the time he'd asked his prom date's father to buy him a six-pack of beer. Of course he hadn't known until later the guy going into the liquor store was his date's dad, but he'd sure felt like an idiot anyway.

"Look, Tom," Lila began, her tone of voice telling him she was going to try to let him down easy.

He didn't want to be let down easy. "Don't say anything, Lila. I'm sorry. I wasn't coming on to you."

She laughed. "You mean telling someone you want to kiss them isn't a come on?"

"I was just being honest." She still wasn't thawing. All the ground he'd gained since asking her for coffee was lost, just like that. "I thought women liked that."

Her lovely dark eyebrows knitted together. "Some women."

Beginning to be exasperated, he sat back in the chair. They'd spent three hours talking without him once suggesting they go to his place, buy condoms, or read to each other from his hardbound collection of Penthouse letters. He hadn't even told her any off-color jokes! And one little comment had straightened her spine like a broomstick down the back of her shirt.

"So you're saying you like lies?"

"I'm saying I don't like to be manipulated." Her voice was flat, and she finally met his gaze fully. "I didn't go to Rivka's show to meet Mr. Right."

The tea was churning a little in his stomach, but Tom ignored it. He usually didn't let even the most foul-tempered people get him riled, but Lila Lazin was managing to push all his buttons. He ran his fingers through his hair, another bad habit to go along with his tendency to blurt out offensive statements.

"Why did you come out with me then?"

She licked her lips, the tiny pink tip of her tongue

stroking the fullness of her mouth in a way that made him want to groan. Lila sighed.

"I had nothing better to do."

Tom shook his head, as if to better hear what she had just said. Not that he really wanted it repeated. He'd heard her pretty plainly the first time.

"Nothing better to do?"

Now she shrugged. "I don't date men like you, Tom. I just don't. I'm sorry. I thought I had made that clear."

He couldn't believe this. All right, so maybe he had been a little spoiled in the past by the women he'd taken out, all of whom had been clearly flattered and excited to date him. Maybe he had grown a little complacent in his appeal. But nothing better to do? She didn't date "men like him?"

"Now we're back to that line." He spoke loudly, as much to watch her blush as anything. He didn't care who turned their heads to look at them in the coffeehouse. He was used to being stared at. And after all, wasn't that what she meant when she said "men like him?"

"Tom!" Lila's whisper was loud and harsh. "Please keep your voice down."

"Sorry, Lila." He couldn't keep the sarcasm from his voice. "I won't waste any more of your time."

He got up from the table, determined to walk out of the coffee house and call it a night. His gut still burned from her words and the bitter tea. "Sensitive," his mother had always called him. "Always taking things too personally."

Well, how was he supposed to take things? He saw an interesting woman staring at him from across the room. He asked her to get some coffee. No pickup lines, no obvious sexual overtures, at least not intentional ones. And what had that gotten him? Insult after insult! So what if her sense of humor had been just weird enough to match his? So what if the sight of her lips made him think about kissing them? To hell with Lila Lazin. He swung open the door and stalked outside. It was three hours wasted, that's all. There were plenty of women who'd love to go out with him. Plenty!

But that's the problem, Tom thought with a half-muttered grumble as the cold wind hit him full in the face. There were too many women who would love to go out with him, but until tonight, there'd been too few he'd wanted to take out.

For a moment, thinking of her soft mouth and the way he knew she'd taste, he almost went back inside. Nothing better to do. Her words echoed in his mind, and he kept walking.

"Tom, wait."

He turned, scowling. Lila hadn't taken the time to fully button her field coat or to pull on her gloves, and she shivered.

"For what?"

"Tom, I'm sorry."

He snorted. "Sure, whatever. See you around."

She followed him to the spot where he'd parked his truck, and stopped him from getting in by placing her fingers on his elbow. Even through the thick leather of his jacket, the touch of her fingers was like a tiny electrical shock against his flesh. He pulled away.

"Tom, I am sorry. I didn't mean to hurt your feelings. It's just that we were having such a nice time, talking and all that. Then when you said that..."

"What, Lila?" His anger began to cool. He turned, shielding her from the wind as best he could. "What was it that upset you? I didn't mean it as a come on. I told you that. I was just being honest."

"Were you?"

That stung. "Of course. C'mon Lila, do I come off like that much of an ass?"

She looked chagrined. "No, I guess not."

The theatre door opened, and they both stepped aside to let a stream of late-night moviegoers shuffle out. The Allen was showing a wildly popular romantic tragedy. A chick flick. One young woman's eyes were so swollen she could barely see, and she still sniffled loudly.

"I meant it, Lila. I still do."

She blinked slowly. She spoke, and her words nearly knocked him off his feet.

"Okay," she said. "Then do it."

Lila couldn't believe she'd said yes, and by the expression on his face, Tom couldn't either. She wanted to laugh, but couldn't manage more than a wobbly smile. Her heart pattered like a thousand tiny Irish step-dancers doing the hora. Her stomach twisted.

Tom just stood there, staring at her. She was wavering between relief and disgruntlement when he stepped forward, grasped her upper arms, and brought his face close to hers. This is it. She hadn't realized she'd closed her eyes in anticipation until what seemed an eternity had passed without her feeling his lips against hers. She opened her eyes to see Tom staring at her, an odd smile twisting the mouth she'd expected to be soft and warm. She stepped back.

"What's wrong?" She was suddenly uncomfortable. It

was one thing to make such an impulsive decision. It was quite another to have to wait so long to fulfill it.

Tom laughed. "Lost my nerve. Not quite the Casanova you were expecting, huh?"

The light shining from inside the coffeehouse painted the right side of his face in varying shades of amber and yellow. The wind had tousled his dark hair into an untidy nest and brought high color to his cheeks. If anything, the dishevelment made him even more appealing.

Tom reached out and grabbed one of her hands, the warmth of his gloves welcome against her bare skin. "Can I try again?"

She shook her head quickly. "No. Now I've lost my nerve."

"So that's that, I guess." He didn't sound completely dissuaded. He tugged her other hand into his own, until they were standing like two children playing London Bridge. "Too bad, huh?"

She laughed again. "Tom, I'm really sorry. I'm a dolt."

He waggled his eyebrows at her. "No argument here."

"I did have a very nice time with tonight. It's just...." She thought for a moment while staring at his face. That beautiful face. "You're too handsome."

He blinked at her, his hazel eyes picking up little bits of golden light from the coffeehouse windows. "Now there's one I've never heard before."

How could she explain herself? "When I saw you tonight at Rivka's show, that's what I thought right away. You're too handsome. You're like some sort of movie star or male model. Not my speed."

Now he frowned, but he didn't let go of her hands. "Lila, I don't know whether to take that as a compliment or an insult."

"I had a really good time tonight," she told him earnestly. "Much better than I've had in a long while. I just want you to know I'm not interested in being some pretty boy's conquest."

She'd hurt his feelings again she saw. This time, he did drop her hands. "What makes you think I'm interested in making you a conquest?"

"I'm no dummy."

"That's what I like about you, Lila. I had a great time with you tonight, too. I meant what I said at the show, that I thought you looked interesting. I was right. So where's the crime in that?"

She sighed. Everything was becoming complicated. "No crime. Tom, believe me, if I were the type of person to just hop into bed with anybody, you certainly would be right up at the top of my list."

"Or a man like me." He mocked her.

She didn't like hearing her own words thrown back at her that way, but he was right. "That's right. A man like you."

"Exactly what kind of man am I?" Tom used his remote to unlock the truck, then opened the driver's door. "Can you tell me that?"

She didn't have a good answer. Tom shook his head.

"I'm used to being judged by how I look, Lila. I'm tired of it, but it's no surprise. I guess I thought there was more to me than just what flesh God decided to cover my skull with. Too bad you can't see it."

He was turning to step into the truck now, and Lila felt instantly, hotly ashamed. Talking with Tom had been wonderful. He definitely had a lot more going for him than just a pretty face. Still, she'd had experience with one modern Adonis not so long ago, and she didn't need another.

"Guys like you don't date women like me." She was desperate to explain and failing.

The wind had picked up even more, now, whipping at the corners of his leather coat when he turned back to look at her.

"You're right, Lila. We don't date girls like you." He slid into the truck and paused before pulling the door shut. "We marry them."

CHAPTER 2

"THE LIGHTING GUY was here this morning, the carpet guy's coming this afternoon, and the plumber will be here tomorrow." Rivka's husky voice filled the telephone clamped to Lila's ear. "It's all coming together, Lila-love. I can't tell you how excited I am."

"Your own gallery." Lila cradled the phone against her shoulder while she signed papers. "Who wouldn't be excited?"

"What do you think we should call it? I was thinking The Gallery on Second."

The gallery was going to be on Second Street. Lila smiled. "Makes sense."

"Or how about The Second Street Gallery?"

"That sounds good, too."

"You're not helping!" Rivka shrieked.

Grimacing, Lila held the phone away from her ear. Darren Ramsey, Lila's personal assistant, took the papers she had signed and slid another sheaf onto the desk. All four of Lila's magazines were due to head to the printer in less than a week. She had a million things to do for each one of them, but she had taken Rivka's call anyway. How could she have refused? She was just as excited for her sister as Rivka was herself.

Giving Darren a thumbs-up to take the last set of forms, Lila mouthed, "My sister." The young man grinned. He'd met Rivka.

"I'll hold your calls," Darren whispered mischievously, ducking out of the office in time to miss being hit full-on by a wad of crumpled paper.

"...a big favor to ask you, Lila-love."

While making faces at Darren, Lila had missed the first part of the conversation. "Sorry, Riv?"

"You know how my mind works, right?" Rivka laughed.

Lila heard the jingle of bracelets. She imagined her sister nervously running her hands through her short, curly hair—a telephone habit she'd had for years.

"The creative part, I mean."

"Nobody knows how your mind works," Lila teased.

"If anybody does, it's you," Rivka shot back, not teasing.

Lila was surprised.

Rivka sounded serious. "You know how I get when I'm in a creative frenzy, right?"

"Sure." Lila's reply was hesitant and a little wary. Rivka was clearly trying to get at something. The question was, what? And what part would she want Lila to play in it?

Though she loved her sister dearly, Lila had no illusions about what Rivka might have in mind. Since they'd been children, it had always been Rivka who'd come up with the seemingly brilliant ideas, leaving Lila not only to do the legwork, but also the clean up. They'd collaborated on everything from lemonade stands to puppet shows, and while many of Rivka's projects had been unquestionable successes, just as many had been dismal failures. Lila had learned to be on her toes whenever Rivka asked a favor of her.

"Remember the treehouse club?" Rivka sounded like a little girl again. "How I thought we could charge admission to the clubhouse to pay for drinks and snacks? And how everybody showed up and paid their quarters, but I didn't have any drinks and snacks to give them?"

Lila laughed suddenly at the memory. "I remember Benny Mason threatening to beat you up, and me running down to the mini-mart to buy some Twinkies."

"You see? That's exactly what I mean. You were always my right-hand woman. You're the one who always took my scatterbrained ideas and made sure they worked."

Lila leaned back in her chair, the magazine production schedule temporarily forgotten. "What are you trying to say, Riv?"

"I have all these great ideas, but when it comes to the follow through...." Rivka laughed again, with no hint of embarrassment. "Except for my paintings, I'm hopeless."

"Yes." This time Lila wasn't teasing. It was true, and they both knew it.

"I want you to take partnership in my gallery. I need someone who I can trust. I need someone who can put up with all my bull and follow through. Will you do it?"

If Rivka had asked Lila to raise her children for her, Lila could not have been more honored. Running Rivka's gallery was in a far different league than running down to the mini-mart to buy snack cakes. This time, her sister had obviously thought about asking for Lila's help.

"You want me to run your gallery?"

"Partnership," Rivka corrected, "but yes."

Lila didn't know what to say. The idea frightened and

flattered her. "I don't know anything about running a gallery, Rivka."

"You don't need to, hon. You just need to know everything about running me."

"What about Mick? Can't he handle it?"

Rivka's snort was so loud Lila had to pull the phone away from her ear. "My Mickey? That blarney-tongued charmer? C'mon Lila! When's the last time I let Mick handle anything but my left—"

Lila laughed out loud. "I get the picture." Mick was a wonderful husband and brother-in-law, but Mr. Responsible he was not. Mick's idea of keeping things straight was knowing which of his guitars needed tuning before he went on stage.

"So you'll do it?"

Although she was flattered by her sister's offer, Lila had been burned too many times by the fire of Rivka's enthusiasm. Honor or no, she wasn't about to agree to the partnership before she'd asked a few more questions. "What do I have to do exactly?"

"Oh, you know. Make sure things happen. Keep my head on straight. Make sure I do what I say I'm going to do. You're good at that."

"Who else is in this partnership?"

"Me and Mick, of course. We're the creative angle, though I can see that causing one of us to sleep on the sofa more than a few times. You know I love my Mickey, Lila-love, but the man can be so stubborn!"

Lila laughed silently. Rivka calling Mick stubborn was the clearest case she had ever seen of the pond calling the ocean wet. The pair of them were both of artistic temperament, prone to the ecstasy and agony of creative successes and failures. Their marriage was one of the most volatile, passionate, yet loving marriages Lila had ever seen.

Still, Lila couldn't help but envy Rivka a little. Her sister had found her soul mate, what Orthodox Jews called the baschert. The one person in the world so perfect for you, no matter how you met, you knew he was the one. Rivka had met Mick at a concert. The Roving Ramblers, Mick's band, were well known throughout the area for their unique blend of traditional Celtic and Cajun music. A slight man with a mop of ink-dark hair and a face creased from smiling, Mick had decided not to return to Ireland after meeting Rivka. They'd been married three months later.

With a sudden shiver, Lila thought of Tom Caine's last words to her. What had he meant by, "We marry them?" Had he been implying something? Obviously not, since he hadn't called her. The showing had been more than a week ago. She hadn't given him her phone number, but when did that ever stop anybody? She was listed in the book. Then again, she hadn't called him either. Lila sighed. She just couldn't seem to get him out of her mind.

"Hello? Earth to Lila Lazin!"

"What?" She was embarrassed to admit she hadn't been paying attention. "What did you say?"

"I'm just telling you who else is in the partnership. Of course, I've asked Martin. He's the business angle. If he can't market my stuff now that I have my own gallery, I don't know who can. Then you, dear sister. You'll be the fire under all our butts, of course. And there's also an investor, for the financial side of it—"

Lila didn't wait to hear about that. "Fire under your butts, huh?"

"Don't get your panties in a twist." The grin was clear in

her voice. "You know you love that stuff. I'll come up with the ideas, Martin will market them, and the investor will pay for them. You just have to be the one who makes sure we all do our jobs on time."

Lila sighed. "It sounds like a lot of work, Riv. I do have a job of my own, you know."

"Ah yes, the high and mighty production manager of Deerkiller magazine." Rivka was teasing again. "And what's that other one? Dollhouse?"

"Archery Hunter and Doll Collector," Lila replied dryly. Her sister knew exactly what she did for a living. "Don't forget Early Colonial Crafts and British Life."

"Will you do it, Lila-love?" Rivka sounded serious. "I don't trust anyone else."

She couldn't say no, and she didn't really want to. Working with Rivka would be as close to being an artist as Lila would ever get. She'd be lying if she said she didn't like being a part of her sister's work. It gave her a taste of what creativity was like.

"I think I'm setting myself up for a whole lot of headaches, but of course I'll do it. When have I ever let you down?"

"Never, Lila-love." Rivka clapped her hands gleefully, like a child. Lila could hear her through the phone. Rivka's bangles clamored and jangled like an out-of-tune calliope. "So you'll be at the meeting tonight, at the gallery? It's Thursday night. You don't have any hot dates tonight, do you?"

Lila flipped through her appointment book. All clear, as usual. She hadn't had a date since she'd gone for tea with Tom Caine. Darn! Now she was thinking of him again. Resolutely, Lila pushed the memory of his face from her mind, though the sound of him saying he wanted to kiss her refused to be banished.

"I'll cancel Keanu," Lila said wryly. Before she could stop herself, she found herself thinking that Tom was handsomer than any movie actor. "Buy me dinner, though."

Rivka chuckled. "No problem. The investor's treating us all to dinner."

"Fair enough. See you tonight."

As soon as she had slung the phone back into its cradle, Lila heard Darren's trademark double tap on the door. Before she could say anything, he'd entered the office with another set of papers filling his hand. He set them down on her desk, then flopped down into the chair across from hers. "What's up with Rivka? How's the gallery?"

"Almost done. She wants me to take a partnership in it."

One of the things Lila appreciated most about Darren was his ability to convey entire conversations with little more than a glance. He was doing it now, she saw, raising his eyebrows and pursing his lips to signify being impressed. He smoothed one coffee-colored hand over his head, tousling the tight cap of bright yellow curls.

"Wow," he said. "That's like her kid or something."

"Yeah, I know."

"The last time my brother asked me to help with anything it was to enter a fantasy football league. As if! Like I care about football." He snapped twice in the air over his head. "Now, if he'd asked me what stockings to wear with the sequined, red cocktail gown, that I might've been able to help him with."

Lila laughed, shaking her head. She knew no one else in the company shared such a casual work relationship with their assistants, but she didn't care. Darren was more than her employee; he was her friend. Some days, he was the only source of humor she had.

"What stockings might that be, Darren?"

"Nude, honey." Darren drew the word out nasally. "Nude."

Rolling her eyes, Lila signed the first paper on the stack. "Darren, you make my life so interesting. What would I do without you?"

Darren grinned. "Spend a lot more time working, less time disco dancin', honey!"

He got up from the chair and did a back-and-forth bump and grind that had Lila giggling like a madwoman.

"Enough!" She glanced furtively out the open doorway of her office. Spying one of the more notoriously nosy coworkers passing by, she made her voice stern. "I'm paying you to make copies and bring me coffee, Mr. Ramsey, not to disco dance!"

Darren grinned. "Shoot, Lila, if you were paying me to dance, you'd never be able to afford my salary."

He's right, too, Lila thought as she scribbled her name on another endless stack of papers. He was good enough to be on stage instead of working behind a desk as her assistant. She'd seen him dance once in a local talent show, and he'd brought the house down.

"I really don't know what I'd do without you, Darren." She was serious.

"If I'm the man in your life, honey, something is seriously wrong."

And the sad thing is, Lila thought as she watched him bump and grind his way out of the office, closing the door behind him, he's right about that, too.

It wasn't that she didn't want a relationship. She just didn't want to date. Living as a single in a couples' world could be hell, but suffering through endless awkward conversations and even worse, uncomfortable silences, had resigned her to ending up old and alone, a crazy lady with fifteen cats.

There hadn't been any uncomfortable silence with Tom. Damn! Lila slapped her signature onto a few more papers, then tossed them in the Out bin. She had to stop thinking of him.

The only thing worse than being an old, crazy lady with fifteen cats would be if she ended up an old, crazy and horny lady. Lila sighed and leaned back in her chair. Horny didn't even begin to describe it. She was flat out sexually frustrated.

And that meant she was thinking about him again.

Damn!

Tom dipped his finger into a vat of tomato sauce bubbling on the stove and tasted it. "Too spicy. Not enough sugar."

The chef, Michel Leroy, nodded. At the moment, his face was as red as the scarf tied around his neck, but his whites were immaculately spotless. He wiped his hands fastidiously on a fresh cloth.

A tall, spare man in his mid-thirties, Michel's thick head of blue-black hair, snapping black eyes, and carefully groomed mustache made him look more like a professional gambler than a chef. He had, however, trained at the Cordon Bleu and was one of the most highly respected chefs in the country. He had come to The Foxfire Pub, he always said, because he was tired of metropolitan life. Harrisburg, Pennsylvania, was the perfect blend of city and country for the French master of cuisine.

Michel may have come to central Pennsylvania to escape the big city, Tom thought as the chef tossed some sugar into the vat of bubbling sauce, but had another reason for staying. Tom's niece, Emma, a fiery, spunky redhead, Michel's junior by at least ten years. Though Michel claimed she drove him insane, Tom thought privately the master of The Foxfire's kitchen was more likely crazy in love. Though the pair was constantly at odds in the kitchen, they managed to turn out some of the area's finest food.

"Oui, sugar. I was telling the sous-chef that very thing, but she...ah! She is not to be listening to me! Forgive me for saying so, Monsieur Tom, but Emma Simmons has no respect for the tomato!"

Tom grinned, but managed to refrain from laughing at the chef's bold statement. He doubted anyone, except perhaps Michel himself, could have any respect for "the tomato." "I'll speak to Emma if you'd like, Michel."

The whip-thin chef's brows knitted into a scowl Tom knew was only partly real. "Oui, Tom. If you would be so kind. I am afraid the sight of her face will have me losing my temper! And anger in the kitchen can come to no good."

The emotional chef was being completely serious. Chuckling, Tom left the kitchen. He'd never seen a person more determined to deny his attraction to someone than Michel Leroy about Emma Simmons. He frowned. Suddenly, he was thinking of Lila Lazin again.

He'd gone home that night with his mind full of her face, her scent still clinging to his skin, the imagined taste of her on his lips. A cold shower had managed to let him sleep, but he'd dreamed about her and awakened, his penis hard and his head swimming. Self-induced chastity was the stupidest thing he'd ever done. Sex was the one thing in life he'd always been sure of. Women—gorgeous, beautiful, hot-bodied women—seemed to fall into his lap without him ever even trying. It was a gift, his grandmother had always said, that face. The best of all the family features tied up in one neat package.

His buddies would think he was crazy if he let on his true track record. He'd hadn't slept with a woman for over a year, when the one-night stand he'd planned to have became an awkward confrontation with a love-starved woman who threatened to slit her wrists because he didn't want to be with her.

Tom didn't know what, exactly, he was waiting for, but the more he tried to put Lila Lazin out of his mind, the more stubbornly she insisted on sticking in it. Her blue ice eyes winked at him from the freezer when he went to do inventory. The complimentary cups of coffee he poured his best customers reminded him too much of her sleek brown curls. The flowers he'd ordered made him think of her fresh, light scent...

It took another trip to the freezer for him to cool off. By the time he gathered the wait staff for pre-dinner instructions, he'd managed to get himself a little bit under control. "Full house tonight, folks. I want to see everyone hopping. You know I won't be here later tonight, so I'm trusting all of you to make things swing."

"I didn't know you liked to swing, Tom." Jennifer, the blonde hostess, gave him a wink. Today she wore a vibrant red suit of some shiny material. Though not inappropriate in any way, the suit still managed to show off a good deal of tanned thigh and bosom. Jennifer's honey-colored hair was swept off her face and emphasized her high cheeks and vivid, cornflower-blue eyes. She was what his buddies would call a hottie.

"Save it for the customers," he told her good-naturedly.

"You're such a flirt," Wendi, one of the waitresses, told Jennifer. She flung her waist-length braid of chestnut hair over her shoulder. The two were best friends.

Jennifer rolled her eyes toward her friend. "And you're not?"

The rest of the staff had drifted away to their other duties. Tom, his mind already on other things, began looking over the list of the night's specials. Emma's homemade gnocchi was one of them, and Tom looked forward to sampling some of it himself.

"We'll miss you later," Jen said.

Tom startled. So involved in the specials, Tom hadn't noticed the tall blonde next to him until he felt her breath on his cheek.

She pouted. "The night shift isn't the same with Frank."

Frank Philips was the night manager. A short, balding man with a wife and six children, he was both personable and efficient. Still, he wasn't exactly Jen's type.

"You'll manage," he told her.

She ran her fingers lightly over his arm. "Where will you be tonight? You hardly ever leave the restaurant on Thursday nights."

Tom shrugged off her grasp. "I have a meeting. Now, Jen, if you don't mind...."

"Sure. Lots of work to do. We know, Tom."

Wendi giggled. "What a slave driver. Don't get out the whips and chains, Tom."

"Wait until after work," Jen added, and the pair finally left him alone.

Watching the two women undulate away from him, Tom, for the first time, found their harmless flirtation annoying. Though he appreciated a beautiful face and body as much as any man, he emphatically did not date employees. Even if that had not been one of his personal rules, Jen and Wendi were too predacious even for him. He preferred to do the pursuing.

Not that it had done much good with Lila.

"I should've kissed her," he mumbled grimly.

But he hadn't kissed her. For some reason, he'd lost his nerve. Staring at her up tilted face, her lovely eyes closed and those perfect lips just ripe and waiting for his mouth to close on hers.... All at once, all he could think about was how much he liked her. She was smart and funny and sexier than any woman he'd been out with in a long time. He wanted to kiss her, sure, but not just standing on the sidewalk. When he kissed Lila Lazin, he wanted it to be in a place and circumstance where a kiss did not have to end the evening.

"'lo, boss," Emma chirped from behind him. Tomato sauce smeared her chin and flour smudged her cheek. Tom could imagine Michel's Gallic shudder at the appearance of Emma's white top, which was spotted with more sauce. "Mike said I was supposed to come and talk to you about the tomato sauce."

Thankful to have his thoughts torn away from the intriguing and annoying Lila Lazin, Tom frowned at the young woman in front of him as sternly as he could. It was a hard effect to master, especially since Emma's green eyes twinkled so merrily. She grinned at him, her freckled nose squinching.

"Too spicy, Emma. You know what I've said in the past about spicy sauce."

"Ah, c'mon, boss." Emma threw up her hands. "Don't you know spice is the variety of life? Or something like that anyway."

Tom sighed, but smiled at Emma. "Do you do this just to get on Michel's nerves or mine?"

Emma squeezed him around the waist affectionately. The top of her head barely reached his shoulders. "Both. It's my mission in life to keep you men on your toes. Besides, adding more sugar would ruin that sauce. How can you put a sweet tomato sauce over my homemade gnocchi? It'd be a sin. A culinary sin."

"Just remember, Emma, you're the sous-chef. Michel is your boss."

"I can get around that," Emma retorted saucily.

"I bet you can."

With just a smile, Emma could have Michel not knowing whether he was slicing or dicing. Tom had seen it more than once. Though they'd never so much as gone on a date, Emma was clearly certain of the chef's romantic inclinations toward her. It was equally obvious to any who knew them that Michel would never admit to such an attraction.

"Boss?"

"Hmmm?" Tom turned back to the specials list.

Thursday nights were Italian night at The Foxfire, with several pasta dishes in addition to Emma's gnocchi featured. Completely involved with perusing the menu, Tom didn't notice Emma's silence until he turned to find her staring at him, bemusement clear upon her freckled face.

"Who is she?" Emma's merry green eyes glinted knowingly.

"Who is who?"

"The bit of fluff who's got you so riled. I could tell something's been on your mind all day. All week, too. You haven't been out of the house except to come to work, and I've actually been able to make a phone call or two. Was it that busty blonde who likes to ride horses? Or the skinny chick who always smelled like gardenias?" She paused, as though a horrible thought had just come to her. "Please don't tell me it's Wendi."

Tom set his jaw. "You know better than that."

Emma sniffed. "Thank God. So who was it?"

Tom shook his head. Emma knew way too much about his social life. He supposed that was the problem when you not only hired your niece as sous-chef in your restaurant, but let her live in your house, too.

"It doesn't matter, Emma. She wasn't interested in me."

Emma stepped back, looking impressed. "Was she blind? I mean, look at you! Every woman who walks in here wants to be on you like butter on a cob of corn!"

"Thanks, Em," Tom replied dryly.

"She really didn't go for you, huh?" Emma appeared sympathetic. "That's a first."

Her casual assessment of his love life suddenly annoyed him. "You make me sound like some kind of Don Juan."

"And you're not?" She raised her eyebrows at him and looked so much like his older sister he might have laughed... had he not been in such a bad mood.

He scowled instead, showing her his back. "No, I'm not. Dating a lot of woman just means I haven't been lucky enough to find the right one yet, that's all."

"Sorry." Emma paused. "I was trying to make you feel better, not worse."

Tom forced a smile on his face for the effervescent young chef. It wasn't her fault Lila Lazin had rejected him. Nor was it Emma's fault he couldn't get Lila out of his mind.

"Thanks, Emma. But I'm fine."

Emma patted his shoulder kindly. "If you say so. If you say so."

Why was everyone so crazed by five o'clock? It made Lila sullen. She lost her parking spot to a pair of middle-aged women driving a Mercedes. She'd had to fight traffic all the way from her office, and now the parking lot was a zoo. Lila swung around the lot again, finally parking so far away from the mall she practically needed binoculars to find the building.

She had some time to kill before the meeting at Rivka's gallery and there was no sense in running all the way home. She'd hit the bookstore. Stephen King's latest novel had just been released, and Lila was aching to get her hands on a copy. She was a manic King fan, devouring his books in hours.

So intent was she on cutting through the crowd toward the bookstore, Lila nearly tripped over a parcel someone had carelessly left on the floor. Biting her tongue as the pain in her toe moved her to curse, Lila stepped back and focused her attention on the package's owner. The petite, platinum blonde glared at her with barely veiled distaste and cradled her violated parcel like it was a wounded child.

"Hello, Lila," the man with the blonde said, his voice so cool it made Lila's arms perk with goosebumps.

"William." She sounded stiff. Her stomach twisted. He looked as handsome as ever, his sandy hair perfectly styled and his fit body perfectly clothed. He still looked as though he could have stepped off the cover of GQ.

"Haven't seen you for a while, Lils." William seemed oblivious to the fact his every word was a sword in her side. He'd even called her Lils, which he knew she hated.

"Well, you wouldn't have, would you?" Lila was glad to

hear that, while William's appearance might be tearing up her insides, her voice remained steady.

William laughed, a completely insincere booming sound. "This is my wife, Pansy." He tugged forward the petite blonde, who stared at Lila as though she had just vomited on Pansy's elegant suede boots. "Pansy, this is Lila Lazin."

"Charmed." Pansy briefly touched Lila's fingers with her own.

"Congratulations," Lila managed to say.

"Thanks." William patted her arm. "You ought to think about tanning. You look like death warmed over."

Then he was gone, taking Pansy with him. Heedless of the crowd surging around her, Lila stared after them until finally someone bumped into her. Realizing she was making a spectacle of herself, Lila sank down onto the nearby bench and forced her hands to stop shaking. The pain had bloomed again with vicious brilliance.

"You're a nice girl," William had said to her—the memory as clear as spring water. He had taken her to dinner at their favorite restaurant. She had thought he was going to propose. Instead, he had broken her heart. "Nice, but not quite enough for me. I need someone a lot...prettier."

Lila had nearly choked on her dinner roll. William's nightmarish words echoed in her head like discordant church bells. "We've been together nearly a year, William. You only decided this now?"

William had smiled, though the expression didn't reach his brown eyes. "It was a kick at first, you know. To see what it would be like to be average. After a while, I just figured I was doing you a favor. I'm tired of doing you a favor."

Incredibly, he had wanted to finish the meal. He had not understood why Lila had left the table, or why she had refused to allow him to drive her home. "After all," he had told her, "it's not like you ought to have believed me when I told you I loved you.

"'That's just what people say," he had said. "My God, Lila, don't tell me you were foolish enough to think a man like me could ever love someone like you."

William had left her shivering in the winter wind outside that restaurant. He hadn't even given her money for cab fare. Lila had walked home. She tossed her pretty shoes in the gutter when one heel broke, and shredded her stockings on the gravel. Her feet had healed, but her heart had not.

Lila sat on the bench for a long time and watched the ebb and flow of evening shoppers pass her by. She didn't want to hurt this much over something as sad and simple as running into an old lover, yet she did. Finally, she forced herself off the bench and headed again toward the bookstore. Not even the heavy novel could lift her spirits.

Thoroughly depressed, she headed over to the new gallery, pausing to put a smile on her face before she went inside. She didn't want to ruin her sister's joy at the new project. The gallery looked gorgeous. Even missing the few final touches that would make it complete, Lila couldn't help being impressed by the building's exquisitely designed interior. Rivka's influence, of course. It was visible in everything from the tiled entryway to the whimsical sunflower-shaped soap dispensers in the restroom.

"Wow," was all she could say when her sister had finished the brief tour. "It's wonderful, Riv. I'm really impressed. It'll be the nicest gallery you've ever shown in."

"I haven't shown you the best part," Rivka said, drawing Lila out of the main space and into a smaller room. "I call this The Bold Room. It's for you, Lila-love."

The rest of the gallery was still empty, waiting for the arrival of Rivka's paintings, but The Bold Room had already been filled. Three walls of the room had been hung with Rivka's canvasses, while the center of the room held only some comfortable chairs.

Paintings of Lila filled the room.

"Why, Rivka?" Lila managed to ask. At the sight of her sister's generous gift, tears had welled in her eyes. She sank into one of the plush seats, unable to keep the grin from bursting through her tears.

"Because I've never devoted a whole show to my paintings of you before."

To Lila's surprise, her normally cheerful sister was teary-eyed as well.

Rivka sat down beside Lila and took her hand. "You deserve this. Without you, I never would've been able to make myself such a success."

"Oh, Riv." Lila tried to wave away her sister's praise, but Rivka refused to let her.

"It's true!" Rivka gave her sister a fierce hug. "You've always been there for me. Whenever I thought about quitting, getting a real job, I could always count on you to talk me through. It was your job at the magazine that kept me in canvas and paints before my first sales. It was your couch I camped on, and Mick, too, when we couldn't afford the rent on our apartment. You haven't done anything but help us out, and I wanted everyone to know that. My sister, the bold."

The sisters shared a sentimental hug before being interrupted by a sound from the doorway. "And sure, if it isn't a fine sight I'm seeing! The two of ya, blathering like a pair of ninnies!"

"Hi, Mick." Lila rose to greet her brother-in-law with a hug and kiss to the cheek. "Isn't this great?"

"Ah, 'tis the best part of the whole damn gallery," Mick said sincerely, his faint Irish brogue thickening noticeably with emotion. "We couldn't've done it without you, lass."

"Don't you start," Rivka admonished, shaking her head. She scrubbed her face free of tears. "You Irish. Ready to cry at the drop of a hat."

Mick pressed a passionate kiss to his wife's mouth. "Ah, go on with you, Rivka Lazin Delaney."

"You didn't say that last night," Rivka countered, squeezing his bum affectionately. The pair giggled and cooed like a couple of teenagers.

They always acted that way, though they'd now been married for almost ten years.

"You've a fine mouth," Mick scolded in jest. "To talk in front of your sister that way."

"Let me show you how fine my mouth is." Rivka countered by kissing him again.

Lila, who was used to the antics of the pair, merely rolled her eyes. She decided to leave them to their mock fighting and look at the room Rivka had named for her. The first painting patrons would see when they entered was the first Rivka had ever done of her, and Lila's favorite. In it, she was sitting in their grandmother's rocking chair—her feet bare and her hair tangled. She was smiling.

It was not only a good likeness, but flattering, too. In it, she looked actually pretty. If only her sister's vision could be what Lila saw when she looked in the mirror every day.

There were other portraits, not all of them Lila as she truly appeared. In some, her features had been blended with those of her mother or grandmother. "Lighting the Sabbath Candles" had Lila clothed in the dress her great-grandmother had worn on her wedding day in Russia, while "Sunday at the Park" showed her as a child. Rivka had painted that one from memory. Finally, Lila had toured the whole room and came to the last.

Titled simply "Lila-love," it showed her standing in front of a bed of flowers, their vibrant colors seeming nearly to writhe off the page. The brush strokes were bold, almost harsh. Thick layers of paint created a three-dimensional look to the piece that was Rivka's signature style.

In the portrait, Lila's arms were raised above her head and her hands stretched toward the blazing orange sun at the top of the canvas. Her face was slightly turned so the viewer could catch only a glimpse of her eyes and mouth. Barely enough by which to identify her, for which Lila was eternally thankful. The portrait was a nude, faithful down to the mole on her right thigh and the way her left breast was slightly fuller than her right.

"Greetings, all," Martin said jovially. A portly, silver-haired man, he always wore an immaculate three-piece suite and had a deep, booming voice. He'd taken on Rivka as a client long before she'd ever gained any notoriety. The Gallery on Second was a much his success as it was hers. "The first meeting of the Delaney Partnership is about ready to roll, eh?"

He joined Lila at the wall. "Brilliance on canvas. Your sister is such a talent, Lila."

Lila blushed, though she knew Martin looked at the picture with nothing more than a practiced art dealer's eye. "She certainly is."

Mick joined them. "'Tis one of my favorites."

Rivka poked his stomach none-too-gently. "Only because it gives you a chance to ogle my sister's goodies, you pervert!"

"Ah, sweetheart, you should know the only goodies I ogle are yours." Mick bent her over for another kiss. Rivka, who knew exactly that, laughed throatily.

Martin ignored them. "We'll just wait for our last partner to arrive."

Lila had the distinct sense Mick and Rivka's antics embarrassed the stately gentleman. She supposed she was so used to their bawdy behavior by now, nothing they did could faze her. After all, when they had all been living in the tiny apartment she'd rented before buying her house, there hadn't been much space for privacy. Lila probably knew as much about her sister's love life with her husband as they did—more than Lila wanted to know anyway.

"He should be here any minute, check in hand." Rivka briefly pulled away from Mick. He wrapped his arms around her and, eyes shining, she leaned into his embrace. "Then we'll officially be in business."

Lila studied the light on Rivka's face. It was her sister's dream come true—her own gallery. Mick stole another kiss from Rivka, and Lila felt a momentary pang she refused to recognize as jealousy. Her sister had it all. A successful career and now her own gallery. And a husband who adored her.

Lila had no more time to dwell on what she may or may not have been missing in her life because the bell on the front door chimed to announce the arrival of the final partner.

"In here!" Rivka called.

"Hello," a masculine voice said, and Lila's heart did a triple-thump.

"I'd like you to meet my sister, Lila Lazin," Rivka said when the tall, dark-haired man had finally made his way to The Bold Room.

Lila could say nothing, could only stare in mingled shock and excitement at seeing him again. He was even more handsome than she remembered, if that was possible. She blushed.

"We've met." Tom spoke wryly. "Hello, Lila."

CHAPTER 3

She was going to die. Explode. Spontaneously combust. There's no way around it, Lila thought. Being this close to Tom was going to send her over the edge.

"Tom, the gnocchi was superb." Martin pushed away his dessert plate and wiped his lips with the fine linen napkin. "And the cheesecake divine."

Tom smiled and shifted his weight, which made his thigh rub against hers. Again. "I'll send your compliments to the chef."

They'd all gone to The Foxfire after the successful gallery meeting, at which Lila and Tom had not had to interact directly. But everything changed when they got to The Foxfire.

Though the restaurant was only a few blocks from her house, Lila had never eaten there before and hadn't realized Tom was the owner. The food was delicious, the atmosphere elegantly casual. Tom had made menu suggestions then left the table a few times to make his rounds through the restaurant. She'd watched him greeting new customers and old alike with the same easy grace. He'd even stopped to admire a little girl's placemat masterpiece, drawn with crayons Tom himself had provided. Lila had to admit she was impressed.

It wasn't until he'd actually sat down to eat with them that the problems began. Lila had been prepared for him to ignore her, especially after the way they'd last parted. He didn't ignore her. He watched her. His eyes caught hers at every opportunity, which, since she wasn't able to stop looking at him, happened a lot. His hand brushed hers "accidentally" when he passed her the butter for rolls she couldn't bring herself to eat. His thigh pressed on hers every time he shifted in his seat. His fingers caressed the back of her neck when he reached behind her to take something Rivka handed him.

In short, the damned gorgeous man was seducing her in front of her sister, Mick and Martin, and not one of them had any clue.

Every time he touched her, it sent a shiver of anticipation straight between her thighs. Lila blessed the thick sweater she wore. It hid the sharp peaks of her erect nipples. She wasn't so pleased with her choice of skirt. It rode too high on her thighs, leaving too much room for air to caress her body in all the ways she was wishing Tom would.

"How was your dessert?" Tom's tone was a trifle concerned. "You hardly touched your plate."

"It was delicious." She hadn't eaten a bite, unable to stop imagining the smooth whipped cream coating Tom's stomach while she licked it off.

Tom's slow smile traveled from his sensuous lips to heat his striking hazel eyes, and the tension rose even higher between them. Why, exactly, had she not wanted to go out with him? Something about him being too good looking? She couldn't really remember. Tom's stare caught her like a stream catches a fallen leaf in its current, and she swirled around and around until she no longer knew which direction she ought to go.

"Well, folks, this old girl's got to roll," Rivka announced suddenly with a loud yawn.

Martin glanced at his watch. "I do as well. It's late. I'd best be getting home. I've got a long drive to North Carolina tomorrow to oversee the packing of those paintings Rivka was showing down there."

Rivka stopped putting on her coat. "Are you ready, Lila?"

She wasn't, but didn't quite know how to say so. "Actually, I'd...."

"Let her finish her dessert," Mick scolded. "Just because the desserts go straight to your thighs, don't deny sweet Lila her pleasures."

Rivka slapped him lightly. "You, my husband, are aching for a breaking. We all came together. Remember? If Lila-love doesn't come with us, how's she going to get home?"

If she had her way, it wouldn't be dessert going straight to her thighs. "I'll walk. You can drop off my car for me later."

Rivka looked doubtful. "If you're sure."

Lila tore her gaze away from Tom's long enough to look at her sister. "I'm sure. Go on. I'd like to eat the rest of this cheesecake."

"All right. Talk to you soon." Rivka pressed affectionate kisses to her sister's cheek and Tom's. "Can't thank you enough, Tom."

Before Lila knew it, the table had cleared and she sat alone with Tom. She glanced at her watch. Martin was right. It was getting late. Not only had their group left, but most of the restaurant had cleared out as well. The staff had already begun putting some of the chairs up on top of the tables in preparation for closing. "I guess I'd better go, too." Lila didn't move.

"I've been thinking about you all week." Tom's voice was so low it was almost as though he didn't want her to hear.

The sweet spot between her legs pulsed, once, twice. "You could've called."

"You didn't give me your number." His voice was quiet, but his eyes were hazel fire.

Her fingers itched to smooth the errant lock of dark hair away from his forehead. His gaze felt heavy upon her mouth. When she licked her lips, the brief tightening of his jaw showed he had been watching her lips.

"Lila, I know I'm not your type of guy. I know we both got off on the wrong foot, but I like you. I'd like to try again. If I wear a bag on my head, do you think you can stand to be seen with me?"

His utterly incongruous statement forced a startled laugh from her. Once out, another joined it, until she had to hold her sides from the force of her mirth. Tom laughed with her, their mingled chortles ringing through the nearly empty room. An oversexed blonde stopped to stare at them with narrowed eyes, but the rest of the staff ignored them.

"Do you want me to call you a cab?" His eyes caressed her mouth, and she licked her lips again just to watch his gaze darken.

"I don't live very far. How about you walk me home instead?"

He reached for her hand and, for one breathless moment, she thought he meant to kiss it. Instead, he used the grasp to pull her to her feet. With no more than a few inches between them, his presence surrounded her like a cloak.

"Only if you promise to invite me in," he said.

"I think I can manage that." Anticipation made her entire body tingle. "I'm ready."

And this time, she wasn't lying.

Tom slapped freezing hands against his sides. "When I promised to walk you home, I had no idea you lived so far away."

Lila laughed. She had a truly lovely laugh, deep, infectious and achingly sexy. Hearing it made him want to sweep her into his arms and kiss the breath out of her...but he held back. Like a long-simmering sauce, there were some things that tasted better the longer you had to wait for them.

Lila patted her stomach. "After that meal, I had to have a long walk. Besides, one more block and we're there."

In the light of the streetlamps, her eyes looked as blue and clear as a spring-fed stream. Her nose had reddened with the cold, as had her cheeks. Her hair had tousled in the breeze and tangled about her face in dark tumble he wanted to straighten with his fingers. It would feel like silk. Feel like silk and smell like heaven.

"You're staring." Unlike the last time she'd accused him of it, Lila didn't look upset.

"I can't help it."

She nodded and smiled, and that tempting pink tongue slipped out to glide along her lower lip again. His groin tightened in response. She pointed to a narrow Victorian house to their left. A solitary light burned in a lower window. As they approached, the porch light also flickered to life.

"That's mine. I have the light on a timer."

He followed her up the front steps, and when she turned to say something, Tom gathered her into his arms and did what he'd wanted to ever since the night of Rivka's show. He kissed her. She stood stiffly in his arms at first, and his first thought was that he'd made another mistake. Then she eased into his embrace like sliding between a set of flannel sheets, and he knew it was all right.

She tasted like cold air with a hint of the spicy sauce she'd had on her pasta. Her lips were soft and warm against his; her tongue a sweet surprise when he urged her mouth open with his own. She twined her fingers in his hair and tickled the sensitive spot at the nape of his neck.

She pressed into his embrace. The bulky field coat she wore obscured any hint of the body beneath it, which was just as well because he needed nothing more to arouse him. He was already hard and throbbing just from the taste of her and the touch of her fingers in his hair.

Lila broke the kiss and stepped away from him. Her blue eyes had grown dark with a passion he was certain he did not imagine. Her perfect lips were swollen from his kiss, a sight that only tempted him to kiss her again.

She smiled. "Hmm."

Nothing more. Just that simple sound of musing. Or maybe she'd said "Mmm," like she'd tasted something good. Either way, the smile and the wordless reply she'd made to his kiss was sexier than any noise he'd ever heard.

He decided on boldness. "Are you going to invite me inside?"

"Yes, Tom." Lila's voice was soft and pitched low, and he heard a note of hesitation in it. Not exactly the tone he'd been hoping for. "I'm going to invite you inside."

Lila led the way into the long hall that stretched the entire length of the house. To the right rose a narrow set of curving stairs. To the left was an arched doorway leading into the living room. Tom followed Lila to the left.

"Make yourself comfortable." She unbuttoned her coat and tossed it over a well-sprung chair badly in need of reupholstering. With her face turned from him it was hard to see if the passion had disappeared from her eyes, but it sure had gone from her voice. "Would you like some tea?"

He didn't, not really, but he said yes anyway.

She moved through the living room and under an arch that led to a dining room. Beyond that was a set of swinging doors into the kitchen. She disappeared behind them and left him to settle himself on the sofa.

The house was decorated simply but with bold taste. Several of Rivka's prints hung on the walls. One in particular caught his eye. "I have this print."

Carrying a loaded tray, Lila returned to the living room.

He smiled at her. "It was the first real art I ever bought. It's my favorite work of your sister's."

She appeared to assess him for a moment. "Is it?"

He moved closer to the wall to look at the picture. "Something about the flowers and the sky makes the rest seem so erotic. The line of the woman's body, the way she's got her hands raised to the sky. It's very sexy." All at once the resemblance struck him, and he felt like a fool. Everything seemed to click at once. The shape of the woman's hands, her hair, the curve of her jaw.

"It's you, isn't it?"

Lila nodded, busying herself with the mugs and spoons. "Yes."

"No wonder I thought you looked so familiar at the show!"

Now she did look up at him. Her brow raised in the look he recognized from the first night they'd met.

"You can't see my face in that picture," she pointed out dryly. "Exactly what part of me did you recognize, Tom?"

Tom knew women expected him to be suave and smooth. Sometimes, he even was. Right now, he felt about as smooth as a gravel driveway on the skin of a toddler's knees. "Your left ear?" He hoped for a smile. To his relief, he got one.

"I don't usually tell people it's me. You're very observant." Lila's expression was inscrutable. She patted the couch next to her. "Sit down?"

He did, remembering the way her thigh had felt against his at the restaurant. What had happened since then? She'd pulled back, was aloof, not like the handful of passionate woman who'd kissed him only moments before on the front porch.

"I had a nice time tonight." Lila poured him a cup of steaming tea. "I like talking to you, Tom."

"I liked talking to you, too." They'd moved from topic to topic like water flowing downstream. Though they'd shared different views on many subjects, not once had either of them gotten defensive or argumentative. Instead, they'd laughed. "I liked kissing you, Lila."

Her cheeks pinked, and her tongue slid across her lips again. "You make me nervous when you say things like that."

"I'm telling the truth."

She looked away from him and toyed with a single curl that had fallen over her shoulder. "I'm finding this all a little weird."

He frowned. "Why weird?"

She met his gaze frankly. "I told you before, Tom. Guys like you don't date women like me."

He smiled. "And I told you—"

She stopped him with a nervous laugh. "I know what you told me."

"Lila, what exactly is a woman like you?"

She shrugged, curling her feet beneath her. "I'm just normal. Nothing spectacular, Tom. A guy like you can probably go out every night with a different woman on his arm and never once have to settle for a date with someone who couldn't pass for a supermodel."

"Do I look like I'm settling by being here with you?"

Again, she shrugged. "Maybe."

"And the kiss? Was that settling?"

"I don't know, Tom!" Lila cried suddenly. "I don't know you at all!"

She was right, of course. They'd spent less than ten hours together in total. Of that, maybe five of those hours they had spent in conversation. Hardly enough time to get to know each other.

"I'd like to get to know you."

"We have nothing in common." Lila winced as the hot tea touched her mouth, and she set her cup down hard enough to rattle it against the saucer.

Tom wasn't willing to let her escape with so feeble an excuse. "What are you afraid of?"

"You." She sounded honest. "I'm afraid of you."

Afraid? Tom frowned as the thought surfaced. Of what? He shifted uncomfortably, unsure of what to do or say next. Had he been too forceful? The privacy that had seemed so seductive before now became awkward. Was she afraid he was going to try to force himself on her?

He knew he was much larger than she was and that made some women uncomfortable. Emma had told him it made them feel at risk. He hadn't understood what it was like to be a woman until his niece had come to live with him. Hell, he still didn't understand what it was like to be a woman. He had an insight, but not much more.

"Is it...am I too big?" he asked, uncertain how to phrase the question.

Lila looked at him goggle-eyed for a moment, a deep, brick red suffusing her cheeks. "What?" Her voice sounded slightly strangled.

"Too big. Do I make you uncomfortable?" The words began tumbling out, a terrible trait he had, but one he couldn't seem to modify. "My niece told me sometimes women are afraid to be alone with big men, that they wouldn't be able to defend themselves if he tried to...if he wanted to...." His voice trailed off self-consciously. "Are you afraid I'm going to try and force myself on you, Lila? Because I would never, ever..."

"Oh, no!" Lila cried, clapping a hand to her mouth—in horror or embarrassment, he couldn't tell which. "Oh, no, Tom, I didn't mean to make you think...."

"I'm sorry if I came on too strong...."

"I wasn't even thinking about that at all...."

They were speaking at the same time. Tom sighed. "You go ahead."

Lila bit her lip and looked at her hands before meeting his eyes. "I didn't mean that kind of afraid."

Now he was even more confused. "What kind of afraid?"

"I'm not physically afraid." She twisted her fingers together in her lap. "To tell you the truth, that hadn't occurred to me at all. I meant afraid. Like afraid...emotionally, I guess."

"Oh." He felt like a jerk, but that's all he could think of to say. His tongue could flap on both sides when he didn't want it to, but just try to come up with something understanding and suave, and he clammed up tight.

"I realize we're not even remotely close to that point yet," Lila rushed on, as if to cover up any embarrassment caused by his tepid response. "I'm not assuming anything, I mean. Not from one kiss. Oh, God." She covered her eyes for a moment. "I'm making a mess of this."

She was and that made him feel much better. At least he wasn't the only one tongue-tied. "No, you're not."

"You really mean yes." Lila gave him a sheepish grin. "I can admit it."

"No, really."

"One thing I respect in a man, above all else, is honesty. I'm making a muck of what I wanted to say. I'm sorry."

Tom did the only thing he could think of to do. He kissed her again. Her mouth had been half-open in speech when he covered it with his, and instantly the taste of her filled him. Her tongue stroked his, then again. His dick stiffened, hard like iron, and he put his hand to the back of her head to pull her closer.

Then all at once she was gone, and the only thing he was kissing was empty air.

Lila got off the couch and knelt in front of the shallow fireplace, well-aware Tom was staring at her like she'd grown two heads or something. She needed to do something to occupy her hands and lighting a fire was the first thing that had come to her mind.

She'd expected him to make some comment, but Tom sat silently. She only had to turn around to look at him, to see his handsome face. Then she'd know whether he was smiling or frowning, whether she'd offended or amused him. Lila wasn't sure she wanted to find out.

The kiss on the porch had taken her breath away and weakened her knees. Clichéd, but true. The kiss on the couch had left her reeling.

As she dropped the matches into the nest of kindling she'd already prepared, Lila noticed her hands had stopped trembling. Good. She needed to have her head on straight, especially if she was going to do what she thought she was going to do.

"I'm not a prude." She kept her eyes focused on the flames. "I've had relationships before. Some have been long, others very short. One night even."

He did not respond. She'd finished the fire, and now could only sit back and watch the blaze fill the fireplace. With one last look to be sure she'd used enough wood, Lila brushed her hands carefully. Then she turned back toward the couch.

Tom had stretched out his long legs and linked his hands behind his head, but at her words, in went the long legs, down came the hands, until he sat straight-backed on the couch, his hands on his thighs.

"Do you want me to leave?"

"No." She put her face on her knees for a moment before looking at him again. "Yes...I don't know."

In one smooth motion, he slipped off the couch to sit by her on the floor. Then his mouth was on hers again, his arms around her, and all she could think of was how good it felt to have the heat of the fire against her back and Tom's heat against her front. She was glad he'd made the move. She didn't have the nerve. In Tom Caine's presence she'd been catapulted back to high school, when the thought of kissing a boy had made her palms sweat.

She was sweating now and not only because the blaze had grown so high behind them. She pushed him gently, meaning to move him a little further toward the couch. At her touch, Tom slid backward onto the floor, taking her with him. She ended up on top of him, their legs tangled, so she became all too aware of the muscles in his thighs pressing against her.

His mouth opened beneath hers and urged her to respond. She did. His tongue swept her mouth, his lips nibbled and sucked at hers. Tom tangled his fingers into the length of her hair and tugged just gently. Lila moaned.

Mortified at the inadvertent noise, she broke the kiss but was unable to pull herself away. Tom's hands clasped her too tightly for that. Her cheeks flushed hotly, matching the heat that had begun to flare in other parts of her body.

"What's wrong?" He didn't let go of her.

Lila managed to slide off his body so she was no longer in full contact. Not that moving away cleared her mind at all. The scent of him still clung to her, and his taste still tingled in her mouth.

"I don't want you to stop."

Tom smiled. "I don't want to stop."

She felt stupid and amorous all at once. Lila shook her head. "I am not in the habit of having casual sex."

But oh, boy, did she want to.

He nodded. "You may not believe me, but neither am I."

She wanted to believe him and searched his face carefully for any sign he might be lying. She saw none, not even the hint of a grin that might show he was being facetious.

"I want you to be sure you know what you're doing."

He chuckled softly. "I'll try my best."

That wasn't what she meant, but she didn't have the willpower to keep arguing. Not with him, and not with herself. She wanted to make love to him. Her desire was an uphill ride on a roller coaster. She wanted to squeeze her eyes shut until the ride was over, but knew she was going to ride the whole way with her hands in the air, screaming with delight.

Tom, thankfully, didn't seem to be as bound into thought as Lila was. He tugged her down to him again, seeking her mouth with a passion she soon eagerly matched. His hand came up to cup her breast through the soft wool of her sweater. Her nipple rose, instantly turgid beneath his fingers.

"Oh, Lila."

The whisper her name on his lips sent a ray of heat directly to her core.

She allowed him to slip the sweater over her head and unhook the simple bra beneath. Her hands went to the buttons of his oxford cloth shirt and slipped them open with far more grace than she expected to have with shaking hands.

His chest was smooth, with just one patch of crisp, curling dark hair in the center. His stomach was ridged with muscle, and another line of the same crisp hair led down past his navel to disappear beneath the waistband of his trousers. Lila wanted to see where that line led. It was the way his hips moved beneath her fingers that prompted her to at last undo the button. His urgency was feeding her own, chasing away the last doubts and reservations she had.

He kissed every inch of her bare skin, moved his mouth along the soft curve of her stomach and smoothed the elastic waistband of her knit pants over her hips. They were both naked before she knew it, and she was on top of him again. His erection nudged her lower belly, and his chest hair tantalizingly scraped at her over-sensitized breasts until, gasping, she had to pull away. The firelight lined him in gold and orange and shone in his hazel eyes. It bathed his body in the colors of autumn leaves.

She sat up, wanting to see all of him. Tom lay back and propped his head on one of the sofa cushions. His gaze caressed her. In the flattering firelight, Lila didn't feel self-conscious. His touch had made her bold at last, and she refused to speculate on whether her thighs looked heavy or her breasts too small.

She took him in her hand and slowly ran her fingers up and down the length of him. His cock thrummed in her grasp, and the sharp intake of his breath made her smile a little.

"Lila." His voice was hoarse, filled with longing.

Suddenly, he tugged her away from him and rolled over her. When she was cradled in his arms, Tom pushed her back gently until her head rested on the cushion. He pressed a rapid line of kisses down over her breasts and stomach. When she saw what he meant to do next, she stiffened.

"Wait." She hadn't prepared for this. Hadn't prepared for any of it, in fact, but the thought of his tongue on her made her feel faint. It would be too much. She would be lost.

He didn't listen to her, pushing away the hand she'd pressed to the top of his head. Firmly but gently, he parted her thighs and pressed his lips to the soft patch of hair between her legs. The pressure of his mouth made her bite back a cry. Then, too soon, he found her clit. Tom first kissed the sensitive spot, then stroked it with the tip of his tongue.

Lila flung an arm across her eyes, unable to watch and not wanting him to see the passion she knew contorted her face. He slipped one finger inside her, and her hips rose helplessly to meet his tongue as it danced along her clitoris. A familiar tension coiled in her belly, growing tighter and tighter until she at last had to gasp his name.

"Tom!" Lila was nearly mindless with the pleasure his tongue and fingers were working on her.

He pulled away, and she found the courage to look at him. His eyes were glazed, but he smiled at her. He moved up to cover her body with his own and pressed deliciously against her.

"This isn't the best time to mention it, but I didn't come prepared for this."

For one moment she had no clue as to what he hinted. Of course. She would have felt like an idiot, if his fingers weren't still tweaking her nipples and making her shift restlessly beneath him. He meant about protection.

"My bag." She pointed. He raised a brow at her, and she recognized her expression on his face. "It's not what you think."

"At this point, Lila, I don't care to think about anything." He rolled onto his back and stretched out one long arm until he snagged the handle of her handbag with one of his fingers.

Lila shuffled in its depths for a moment and pulled out the small container that had once held a travel-size pack of disposable wipes. She opened it and took out the small foil package. Just because she wasn't in the habit of picking up men didn't mean she intended to ever be unprepared.

Tom didn't let the moment turn awkward. Deftly, he took the condom from her and opened it, slipping it on with no self-consciousness at all. Then he was on top of her again, kissing her mouth and neck, whispering her name over and over.

"Thank you." Lila was glad he hadn't made an issue of wearing the condom, and even more relieved she'd had one available.

Tom propped himself on his elbows and searched her eyes. "Are you sure you want to do this?"

She had never been more certain about anything. She had never wanted a man so badly. "Yes."

He reached his hand down between their bodies—his palm brushing once more against her in just the right spot. Then he had positioned himself and was inside her with a smooth, gentle motion that made her moan aloud.

She wasn't embarrassed this time. Tom answered with a soft groan of his own. Lila reached up to wrap her arms around his back, running her fingers over and over the smooth skin and down to the first curve of his strong buttocks. They clenched beneath her touch as Tom set a slow, strong rhythm of thrusts.

The pace quickly became faster as she urged him on by pushing upward with her hips. With every thrust, he rubbed against the most sensitive part of her. He buried his face in her neck, both of them moving in tandem.

Her climax was perilously close. The scent of him washed over her and mingled with the fire's smoky smell. They were moving together in perfect harmony, so perfect tears sprang to her eyes with the intensity of her coming orgasm.

"Lila."

The sound of him whispering her name pushed her over the edge. Her nails dug furrows into his back as the ball of sensation inside her compressed further and further until, at last, it broke apart with a shatter. Splinters of ecstasy filled every part of her.

Above her, Tom made a soft cry through clenched teeth

and captured her mouth again. When he pulled away, it was to bring his face to hers, to look deep into her eyes. He thrust a final time inside her and shuddered. She felt the throb of his climax inside her, and it sent her once more into spasms of rapture.

Tom held onto her so tightly, she was almost unable to breathe. Lila found she didn't care. In his arms, she had never felt more wonderful.

CHAPTER 4

STEAM FILLED HER NARROW SHOWER, wreathing him in fog, but Lila couldn't miss the gleam in Tom's eyes. The water cascaded over his dark hair and smooth skin, and Lila put up a hand to brush his bangs out of his eyes.

"That's a devilish look." Lila let her fingers slide across his cheek and down to cup his jaw. He tilted his head and caught her fingertips in his lips and sucked gently, sending a thrill of sensation through her body.

Tom cupped one breast, letting his palm caress her erect nipple. "Me? Devilish? Nah."

His hand felt so good she arched her back to urge him silently to caress the other one, too. He did without hesitation, then pulled her closer and let his soap-slippery hands glide over her skin. He bent to kiss her while the water pattered down all around them, and she closed her eyes to keep the spray from blinding her. They'd kept the bathroom lighting dim, and now, with her eyes shut, Lila's world became heat and water, and Tom's hands on her skin, his mouth on hers. The stiffness of his erection stroked her belly, and she parted her thighs to let him rub against her there. His hands found her buttocks and held her close.

He left her mouth to kiss and nibble along the curve of her jaw and then to her neck. He found the super-sensitive spot at her neck and shoulder, which made her wiggle.

"Careful," he warned. "Don't slip."

Lila opened her eyes. "This shower is so tiny I don't think there's room for me go down."

She'd meant her words to have a double meaning, and waited for his reaction. William had never "gotten" jokes like that—but Lila firmly put William from her mind. Now was not the time. Tom grinned and gave a pointed glance toward the floor.

"Too bad."

Lila let her eyes slide coyly along his torso, down to where his erection jutted up between them. "Then again, maybe I can find a way."

She knew she didn't imagine the flicker in his dark eyes. Tom swallowed so hard she saw the bob of his Adam's apple, and then he licked away the water from his lips. "Maybe you can."

Never taking her eyes from his, Lila dropped slowly to her knees. The cushioned bath mat kept her knees from hurting as she settled herself. Now his cock was at eye height, and though the lighting was dim, Lila had no problem seeing all Tom had to offer.

His penis was just as perfect as the rest of him. She'd never much cared about length and girth, as long as the unit in question was put to good use, but there could be no complaining about the size and shape of his erection. Soft, curly hair, as dark as that on his head, surrounded the base and tufted the scrotum beneath. If there'd ever been a more perfectly proportioned prick, Lila had never seen it, in real life or in pictures.

For a second, a wave of self-doubt washed over her. The man in front of her was truly an earth-bound god, sheer physical perfection, any woman's dream come to life. The sex downstairs had been fast and hard, but glorious, and she had no doubts that the sex in the shower was going to be just as fantastic.

So, why was he doing it with her?

"Lila? Are you all right?"

She looked up to see him looking down, standing so the curtain of water parted around them and didn't splatter her in the face. "I'm fine."

"You don't have to, if you don't want to."

He meant using her mouth, she realized. Lila blinked and shook her head. "No, really, I'm fine."

The fact he'd been willing to forgo this pleasure if it made her uncomfortable made her more interested in providing it. She smiled, forcing herself to put away the doubts and enjoy the moment, however brief it might turn out to be. "Fair's fair, Tom."

He grinned and put his hand on her head. "Only if you want to."

She answered him by taking him into her mouth as far as she could, which proved to be all the way. Looking at his erection, she'd thought there would be no way she could possibly take him so far without choking, but this proved again how perfect he really was. She slid him out, then in again, concentrating on giving him the same amount of pleasure he'd given her downstairs.

His groan and the way he wrapped his fingers in her hair rewarded her efforts. The sound of his arousal fanned her own, and Lila slipped a hand between her legs to stroke herself while she sucked him. His strong thighs bunched and flexed as he began to thrust. Her hand moved faster, fingers sliding over her erect clit, already slick with her own juices. The pounding of the water around them merged with her rhythm and the beating of her pulse in her ears, like music.

Orgasm rippled through her, making it hard to keep a steady pace, but Tom didn't seem to notice. His thrusts had become ragged, his moans louder, and when he said her name it sent her crashing over the edge. She lost her grip with her gasp of ecstasy, and his cock came to rest, hot and throbbing against her cheek. She grasped it with her other hand, stroked, once, twice and he spasmed in her palm.

The world swam from the heat and steam and the force of her climax, and Lila had to blink and take a deep breath to clear away the threatening faintness. Tom leaned over her, hands braced against the small shower stall's back wall, feet pressed against the front wall. She still held him, and she took him into her mouth again, alternating with her lips and fingers until he cried out hoarsely.

Another small burst of climax made her clit throb and she answered his cry with one of her own. He sighed. His body relaxed.

It took her a minute to notice his teeth were chattering, and to feel the water had gone ice cold. His body had shielded her from the frigid spray. Chagrined, Lila got to her feet and reached for the faucet, then grabbed a towel and held it out to him.

"Ran out of hot water," Tom said unnecessarily as he rubbed his face dry, then peered at her over the top of the towel. His eyes twinkled. "Probably about five minutes ago."

Lila laughed. "You should've said something."

"Couldn't speak." He shrugged and wrapped the towel

around his waist, then pulled her close for a long, lingering kiss. "I was busy thinking about something else."

She stepped back from his embrace, wrapped her own towel around her and squeezed the water from her hair. "Your lips are blue."

If he noticed her hesitation, he didn't say anything. Instead, Tom went to the sink and filled his palm with some water, then drank it. He stretched out his arms, which looked impossibly long in her small bathroom, then turned and faced her with the same devilish grin he'd given her earlier.

"I think I could use that hot tea you offered earlier."

She put out a hand to touch his goose-pimpled arms, then shook her head and laughed again. "I think I can boil some water. Why don't you get dressed? You'll be warmer that way."

Despite the two fabulous bouts of sex they'd just had, walking around naked in front of him was a little too nerve-wracking. Tom tilted his head and pursed his lips, like he could tell the real reason she was suggesting he get dressed, but he nodded anyway. He ran his hands through that dark, silky hair, bent as though to kiss her again and nodded slightly when she turned her head so he met her cheek instead of her lips. Then he left her alone in the bathroom, and Lila pulled on her robe to go downstairs and make the tea. She studiously avoided her face in the mirror, not sure she wanted to see her own expression.

Lila woke to the sound of pans clattering from downstairs in the kitchen. At some point during the night, after the caffeine from the tea had worn off and the conversation faded into yawns, she and Tom had climbed the narrow stairs to the comfort of her room. Sleeping with him had been an uneasy luxury. While having his arms around her as she slipped into sleep had been lovely, waking to find his elbow in her ear had not.

Rolling over, she pressed her face against the pillow he had used. The scent of him still clung to the fabric, and she decided she wouldn't wash the case until his smell faded. Nothing like acting like a junior high student, she scolded herself, but then snuggled into the pillow again.

She'd expected to feel awkward after making love. She'd assumed Tom would leave with some excuse about having early morning plans. She'd thought talking with him after they made love would no longer be as easy and comfortable as it had been before. She'd been wrong about everything. Tom made her laugh, which was more than any man had done for her in quite a while.

The sex had been great, but Lila discovered the conversation after had been even better. She'd pretended for a long time that being alone didn't matter to her, for so long she'd forgotten how nice it was to sit with a man on her couch and watch the fire burn without having to make small talk.

More than just a one-night stand. The thought startled her into sitting up. She scrubbed at her face and rubbed her eyes, then crossed her arms over her chest. What was she thinking? Lust had gotten the better of her intellect last night, but in the light of day, she had to be smarter than that. She knew it was impossible Tom Caine could be anything more than just a fling. A man like him wouldn't be satisfied with her for very long, and Lila had no intentions of setting herself up for more heartache. They'd had some great sex. He was eye-candy. He'd given her multiple orgasms, but that didn't mean they were destined for...

For what?

Lila sighed, listening to the intriguing clang of pots and pans from downstairs. She'd had exactly one one-night stand in her life, and that had been unintentional. The experience had been so horribly, awfully bad she'd never gone on another date with the guy, who'd turned out to be a bigoted, self-righteous jerk. It had been a mistake.

Making love to Tom wasn't a mistake, she knew. But believing there could be anything more out of this was. Lila shook her head to clear it of the late-night cobwebs. He was a nice guy, great in bed, but he got up way, way too early in the morning. And he stole the covers. And he left wet towels on the floor.

There. She'd thought of sufficient reason to convince herself that sex was all this was, and all it could be. Hadn't she? I have to, she thought firmly. Bargain basement grab bags and all that stuff, remember, Lila? Remember William? And with that thought to sober her, she got out of bed and went downstairs.

She found the small table expertly set with the full array of her nicest dishes, silverware, and glasses. A vase held a single red rose. It was the velvet one that had come off the box of Valentine chocolates Darren had given her last February, but she smiled anyway.

Tom turned from the stove. "Just in time. Food's almost ready."

He wore a pair of her fleecy sweatpants. Borrows clothes without asking. Another reason not to get hung up on this guy, she thought. While she swam in the heavy material, the pants fit his rear end snugly enough to nearly be obscene. He'd wrapped one of her aprons around his waist, but his chest was bare. She noticed the marks her nails had made in the tawny skin of his back and fought back a blush. No use in acting the coy maiden. Not after last night.

"Smells delicious." Lila slid into a chair and found a mug of hot tea waiting for her. He'd put in sugar and just enough cream to turn the tea a caramel color. He'd remembered how she liked it. "Usually on work days, I just grab some cold cereal, so this is a real treat. What's on the menu?"

"Omelettes à la Caine." Tom flipped the pan expertly to cook the eggs evenly. "Onions, green peppers, some garlic...."

Lila groaned. "I'm starved."

Tom slid an omelet onto each of their plates and sat down at the table. "I was going to make a western omelet, but you didn't have any ham. So I substituted."

Lila paused from drinking her tea. Here it comes. The Talk. "I don't eat pork."

Tom paused from cutting into his omelet. She could practically see the gears grinding in his mind as he thought about her name, the subject of her sister's paintings, perhaps the gold-and-brass menorah on her mantelpiece. As Lila watched, a slow flush crept into Tom's cheeks. He looked as comfortable as a man sitting on a cactus.

"I'm Jewish."

He nodded. "I should've known."

Now she began to feel uncomfortable. "Should I have told you? We didn't talk about religion, Tom."

For the first time since knowing him, awkward silence hung between them. She took a sip of her rapidly cooling tea. Tom cleared his throat.

"Does it matter?"

Lila met his gaze levelly. It would not have been the first time a man had lost interest in her because she didn't celebrate Christmas. If her faith was going to be a problem, best she learn now. "You tell me."

He shook his head and laid his hand across hers. "Of course not. I just feel stupid about the ham comment. I'm sorry."

More relieved than she cared to admit, Lila squeezed his fingers. "Let's not ruin a perfectly wonderful night by worrying about stupid things."

He lasciviously waggled his eyebrows at her. "It was pretty wonderful, wasn't it?"

"Of course it was." Lila grinned. "I mean, look at you! You're gorgeous! How could it not have been?"

His flirtatious grin faded abruptly. He pulled his fingers out of hers. Tom gave her a crooked smile. "So...dinner tonight?"

"Oh...I'm sorry. I can't." It wasn't a lie. She had an eye doctor appointment.

His gaze flickered. "Tomorrow? Lunch?"

She knew he was waiting for her to tell him yes, but the words didn't seem to want to come out. She bit her lip, tried to speak, but could only make an awkward squeak.

Tom got up from the table and left his omelet uneaten. "I think I'd better go."

"Wait." It was too late. His expression told her no matter what she said, she'd only be making matters worse. "Tom. Please."

"I'll see you around." Tom's voice was cold as he tossed the apron onto the back of the chair. "Don't bother to get up. I'll find my own way out."

The slamming of the front door was like a blast of dynamite. The house felt suddenly much emptier, as if by Tom's leaving he'd taken something vital with him. Lila stared at the remains of her omelet and felt very small.

Tom was furious. What's more, he felt...used. A sensation he'd never before had the pleasure of experiencing, though he was guiltily certain he'd been the cause of it in more than one woman.

Lila wasn't the type to hop into bed with anyone, he reminded himself. But if she was, it would be with a man like him. The words had come straight from her mouth. It all came down to the same thing again. His face. His body. All the things God and fate had seen fit to grant him with no effort on his part. Not his level temper or sense of humor, or even his successful business. None of that had mattered. What upset him most of all was he had thought he and Lila had made a connection beyond the physical. Obviously, he was wrong.

"'Morning, boss," Emma greeted Tom as he slammed through the front door. "Have a nice night?"

She must have guessed the answer by his stormy expression because the grin on her freckled face was replaced by a look of concern. "You okay?"

He gritted his teeth "Fine."

"Woman trouble?"

Tom glared at her. "The last thing I want to do this morning is discuss my love life with my niece. I'm going up to take a shower. Then I'm going by the restaurant."

Emma let out a slow whistle. "Woman trouble, all right."

Tom ignored her, instead climbing the wide-set stairs two at a time. Tom entered the bedroom, tossed off his coat, and pulled his shirt over his head. Then he realized he was still wearing the fleece pants he'd borrowed from Lila.

Sinking into the overstuffed chair in the corner, he sat with fists clenched on his thighs. His stomach churned fiercely. Never had a woman knocked him so low with such a casual comment.

"Damn!"

The invective only made him feel slightly better. He tried a few more, growing progressively fouler until last he'd exhausted his store of creative curses. He still felt lousy.

He'd started the day feeling so great. Tom had never quite learned how to wake up with a woman in his arms. Yet, with Lila it had just seemed natural. It had seemed impossible to do anything else.

His fists unclenched. True, they didn't seem to have much in common. Everything from their taste in movies to the brand of cola they drank was different. Yet, talking to her had been as satisfying as making love to her had been. He could have talked to Lila for hours or sat silently with her for just as long and never become restless.

Tom had never really been in love, though he'd said the words perhaps half a dozen times. He'd never fallen hard for any woman before, preferring instead to remain commitment-free. It wasn't that he'd been concerned about keeping himself open for something better to come along, as most of his buddies were. It was more that no woman he'd ever dated had ever bothered to look beyond the face and body, which, until last night, had been fine, since he'd been doing pretty much the same.

Lila had led him to believe she'd made love to him in spite of his face, not because of it. She'd really fooled him, made him a fool. The sooner he forgot about her, the better off he'd be. But damn! Why did it have to make him feel like his chest was filled with broken glass?

The wildflowers in Lila's hand were an explosion of expensive, off-season color. Vibrant, brilliant purple mingled with golden yellow, fiery orange, and stunning red. A single white rose centered the bouquet and gave it the touch of class Lila wanted.

The Foxfire was busy with its lunch-time crowd. Mothers with toddlers in strollers sat next to business-suited executives and denim-clad college students. The place was packed. Great. Just what she needed—an audience to her folly.

Lila took a deep breath and clutched the bouquet in front of her like a shield before she pushed through the frosted glass door. Only when her fingernails began cutting into her palm did she notice how tightly she held the flowers. She forced her fingers to relax.

"One for lunch?" The hostess was the same tall, cool blonde whose makeup looked like it had been applied with an artist's brush. Every feature was lined or enhanced, but so subtly it was difficult to pin the effects on rouge or eyeshadow. She made Lila feel like she'd rolled out of bed without bothering to brush her hair or her teeth.

"Actually, I'm here to see the owner."

The hostess blinked twice and looked at Lila with new eyes. Her liquid green gaze took in the flowers, and a tiny smile tugged the corners of her freshly glossed lips. She tapped her perfectly manicured talons against the lectern. "I'm not certain he's available right now. Is he expecting you?"

Though she thought violent behavior crass and cheap, Lila wanted to slap the smile off the other woman's face. She could tell what the blonde was thinking just by the bemused smirk. She had seen it before, on the women who knew William.

Just to spite the other woman, Lila wanted to respond coolly, that yes, Mr. Caine was expecting her. Of course he was. In fact, he had begged her to visit him over the lunch hour.

"No, he isn't." Lila couldn't say anything else. Tom hadn't begged to see her. She hadn't even heard from him in four days. After what she'd said, he probably didn't want to see her.

"I'll see what I can do." The hostess left her post in a swirl of musky perfume.

She should just turn around and leave. She'd only come here because she couldn't stop thinking about him. Every night before she went to bed, his was the last face she saw. Every morning, the fact he wasn't there beside her made her stomach hurt.

She'd never obsessed about a man before. She'd never had to close her eyes against a sudden memory of his face or the way he smelled. She'd never had to whisper his name to herself in the mirror simply because she so badly wanted him beside her. Not even William had filled her head the way Tom did.

It was lust and nothing more. An itch that should have been scratched on Thursday night. But if that was true, why had she bought flowers? Why had she dialed his number half a dozen times and hung up before the first ring? Sex could be a very powerful motivation for action, but this went beyond two people going to bed. She needed to apologize to him because the thought she had hurt him made her ache inside.

She turned to go, unable all at once to face him with so much emotion battling inside her. He would not be home at this hour. She could call his house and leave a message. She could write him a note and mail it so she wouldn't have to speak to him at all...

"Lila?"

Oh God. Lila turned, her hands suddenly trembling. "Hi."

He looked at her warily. Coolly. The way he'd looked when he left her house. Blindly, she thrust the flowers at him.

"These are for you. I just wanted to say I was sorry. I'm such an idiot. This isn't the place. I'm sorry."

Thankful the all-knowing hostess hadn't been there to see her act like such a fool, Lila headed out of the restaurant. His voice stopped her before she could reach the door. She paused without facing him.

"Nobody ever gave me flowers before."

She looked back at him and discovered, to her sudden dismay and mortification, tears had welled up in her eyes. She blinked them back. She didn't want to cry. Not here, of all places. Not in front of him.

"I thought you might like them. They're a little wild, and they smell good. Like you." She was babbling now. Heat rose in her cheeks. This was worse than anything she'd imagined.

Tom stepped forward and took her arm. "Let's go into my office."

He walked her quickly back through the restaurant and skillfully steered her around any obstacle, which was good since now the tears in her eyes were blinding her. He opened a door and gently pushed her inside.

"Why did you come here?" Tom led her to a soft chair.

Lila pressed her cool hands against her flushed cheeks. Deep breath in, deep breath out, until the tears no longer threatened. She looked at him.

"I wanted to apologize for what I said on Friday morning. I was stupid. I'm sorry I hurt you."

"What makes you think you hurt me?" Tom leaned back

against the desk. With his arms folded across his chest and his long, long legs crossed at the ankles, he wasn't exactly a picture of welcoming warmth. "You can't hurt someone who doesn't care about you." His hazel eyes were stormy, his lips a thin line.

His words slapped her. Lila blinked, and the heat disappeared from her face instantly, as though she'd just plunged into an ocean of ice. "I see." Her back stiffened. Once again her fists clenched until her palms ached from the press of her nails against the flesh. She rose to go and did not look at him. If she looked at him, she might slap him or cry and she wanted to do neither.

"Do you?" Tom stepped closer to her and caught her arm to prevent her from leaving.

She pulled her arm from his grasp. "Yes, I think I do."

"I don't think so." He towered over her. "I said you can't hurt someone who doesn't care about you, Lila."

She whirled on him, sudden fury rising in her like a tidal wave. "I heard what you said, Tom! I understand!"

The hands that had worshipped her flesh now gripped her tightly enough to hurt. Refusing to wince, Lila tried to pull free. Tom wouldn't let her.

"You did hurt me." He moved his face closer to hers, and his voice almost became a growl. His eyes were inches from hers, and she could see flecks of gold glittering in the amber-green depths. It took Lila a moment to digest what he'd said. As the fight faded out of her, Tom let go of her arms. He rubbed his fingers up and down along where he'd gripped her to ease the sting.

"I do care." Tom paused as if to gather his courage. "Why did you come here?"

"To say I was sorry."

He pulled her to him and sought her mouth. She met

his kiss eagerly. When he urged her lips to part, she did that, too. His hands crept up to tangle in her hair, and she didn't protest. It was all she'd wanted him to do, since the first time she'd seen him. All she'd thought about.

"So now what?" Tom pulled away from her.

"I like being with you. Can we leave it at that for now?"

He shrugged. "If you insist."

Lila gently disentangled herself from his grasp. "I've got to get back. I have a thousand things to do this afternoon."

"When can I see you again?"

"You'll see me tonight," she reminded. "We have a partnership meeting at the gallery. We're supposed to be planning the gala opening."

Tom mock-slapped his forehead. "I forgot. I'll be there."

They stared at each other in silence for a minute. Then Lila reached up to peck his cheek. Tom captured her shoulders and refused to release her until she had kissed him as passionately as before.

"I'd better go." Lila laughed again.

"I'll see you tonight."

At the thought, her belly quivered. Tonight, indeed.

The rest of the day passed in a daze for Tom. He placed three incorrect orders for produce before Emma finally took over. Ordering him out of the kitchen, she grabbed the order book from his hands and shook her head.

"Boss, go put your flowers in a vase before they wilt," she ordered. "Better yet, go home and take a cold shower."

Only a niece who was practically like a younger sister could get away with telling him what to do. Tom didn't care. Lila had brought him flowers. Nobody had ever brought him flowers, and though he knew his buddies would make unrepentant fun of him if they found out, it would mostly be out of jealousy. Nobody had ever brought them flowers either.

"You're in a good mood." Jennifer paused to stuff a handful of menus into a drawer. Now that lunch was over, The Foxfire would be fairly quiet for a few hours until dinner. She and Tom had often spent the time talking.

Not today, though. Visions of dark curls and blue-ice eyes were filling Tom's mind. Visions of Lila.

"I'm in a great mood." Tom punched the air.

Jennifer smiled flirtatiously. "How come?"

"No reason."

She must have caught the unspoken answer in his voice. She frowned, an expression that didn't flatter her. As if realizing that, she made an obvious effort to smooth the lines of her face into a smile.

"Well, if you're in a good mood, so am I," she cooed.

"Good. Then you won't mind working the dinner shift tonight. I've got to get home early. I've got a date tonight."

It was a good thing he'd been out of range of her nails, he thought as he pushed through The Foxfire front doors. Otherwise, Jennifer might have given him a pretty bad scratch. He laughed about it on the way home, but realized how much had changed in the past few days. Even as short as a few months ago, he'd have returned Jen's flirting without thinking twice. They'd never dated, though she and Wendi had sometimes ended up at the same local watering holes he'd used to frequent regularly. It hadn't been hard to see that the hostess and the waitress would have gladly gone home with him, but he'd never taken it that far.

And now, he never would. He laughed again as he pulled into the driveway. *She brought me flowers.*

Investing in Rivka Delaney's art was the best decision he'd ever made. The afternoon took forever to drag by, but at last it was time to head over to The Gallery on Second. Parking his hunter-green Chevy Tahoe in the back lot, Tom let himself into the gallery with the key Rivka had given him. The lights were dim, but he heard voices from the back.

"Tom!" Rivka rose and kissed his cheek. Mick and Martin stood and shook his hand. Tom turned to Lila, who smiled and gave him a quick peck on the cheek.

"Not in front of my sister," she murmured into his ear. "She doesn't know."

"We were talking about the opening night party." If Rivka had guessed anything about her sister and Tom, she didn't let it show. "I want it to be the best party this town has seen in a long time!"

"She wants to make it a costume party." Lila raised one eyebrow. "Sort of a masque."

"Lila-love's not thrilled, as you can tell." Rivka nudged her husband. "But we love it, don't we, Mickey?"

"You love it because you want to dress like a sheik and a harem girl." Lila rolled her eyes.

Rivka rolled eyes shaded in spangled eyeshadow. "So? What's so bad about that?"

Martin cleared his throat and cut off Lila's response. "A costume ball would certainly attract the right people. The mayor always attends the Art Council's annual masquerade."

"So, a masque it is!" Rivka clapped her hands and shot her sister a triumphant look. "Tom, what do you think? It's mostly your money after all."

"If it's what you want, Rivka, go for it," Tom replied gallantly. "You're the artist."

"See?" Rivka stuck her tongue out at Lila. "Tom likes my idea."

Lila raised her hands helplessly. "All right, you win. But I'm choosing my own costume."

The last time Lila had gone to a costume party, Rivka had insisted on costuming her. Lila had spent the entire night in the bathroom, scrubbing off the silver paint that was giving her hives. A lovely water nymph she had been...not.

"Fine...whatever." Rivka waved her hand airily. Her bracelets jangled. "Come as Gumby for all I care."

Tom wouldn't mind seeing Lila in a harem girl costume. As if she could read his thoughts, Lila caught his glance and smiled. The smile lit up her eyes and suddenly had him wanting to bend her over the table and make love to her right there.

"I wanted me and the boyos to make the music," Mick said. "But my Rivka says she can't have me away from her side."

Rivka shook her head. "I'll be too nervous. We'll have a DJ. I need you with me, Mickey."

Martin smoothed graying hair. "I've already made arrangements for the paintings to be hung. We'll have all of Rivka's originals here, even some which have been purchased. The owners have agreed to lend them for the night. Of course, we'll also be offering all her prints for sale. We're going to have a drawing to win one of her latest portraits, too."

"It's going to be fantastic!" Rivka let out a little scream. "I'm so excited!"

Lila laughed at her sister's antics, but didn't resist when Rivka leaned over the table and gave her a hug. Watching them, Tom noted how much they looked alike.

"The Foxfire is going to do the food, right?" Rivka turned to Tom.

"Sure."

"Can you and Lila take care of that? I think you two will work great together."

If only she knew. "I think we can manage that. Lila?"

Lila bit back a smile. "Oh, I'm sure we can come up with a lot of interesting ideas."

Rivka looked back and forth between the two of them as if she sensed an undertone to their conversation but didn't know what it was. "Great. I'll leave you to it then. Don't worry, Lila-love. It won't be hard."

Lila seemed to be stifling a giggle. "That would be too bad."

Rivka peered at her sister. "If I didn't know you better, Lila-love, I'd say you were making a dirty innuendo."

Lila returned her sister's look with exaggerated innocence. "Me?"

"Don't worry, Rivka." Tom gave Lila a steady gaze. "I'll keep your sister firmly in hand."

Now Rivka turned to look at him with narrowed eyes. "What's going on between you two?"

"None of your business." Mick gave her a stern look. "Leave them alone. They're jesting with you."

Rivka appeared about to say more, but her husband silenced her with a kiss and a squeeze.

"All right! Meeting adjourned. I just remembered some business we have at home."

The meeting was over, just like that. Rivka and Mick cleared out like their tails were on fire, and even Martin left with little delay. Promising to lock up, Lila and Tom were the only two left in the gallery.

"So," she said slowly. "Do you want to talk about food?"

The tension was nearly visible in the air between them.

"I'd like to talk about eating."

"Why talk?" Lila's eyes were aglow with blue ice and her voice a husky intimation. "When you can do?"

Then there was nothing more to be said.

CHAPTER 5

The caramel wasn't hot enough to burn her skin, but Lila definitely knew exactly where Tom was dripping it. It made a sticky puddle on the soft curve of her stomach and oozed lazily down her sides. The more she wriggled, the faster it slid across her skin. Unfortunately, the things Tom was doing to her with his hands and mouth made it impossible for her to stay still.

"Now for the best part," he murmured and paused in his exploration of her body to reach for the cardboard container beside him.

She nearly shrieked as the ice cream landed first on one breast, then the next. Her nipples rose like iron spikes. Lila let out a wheezing, shuddering laugh at the sensation.

"It's cold!" Her complaint wasn't very fierce. The frosty dessert was already melting on her passion-heated skin. "When you made me promise not to move, you didn't say anything about freezing me to death!"

"I told you I wanted to make upside-down sundaes and you agreed." Tom bent his head to suckle the dripping ice cream off her nipples. "First we did the cherry, then the whipped cream. Then the caramel...."

She forced a solemn expression to her face. "Then the ice cream. You've made a mess of me."

The glint in his eye promised lust. "I'm going to clean it up. Starting right now."

True to his word, Tom moved his mouth along her entire body and paused at every place he had dripped or slathered with food. First, he suckled and laved her breasts and nipples clean of vanilla, moving from one to the next until she had to physically clench her hands together to keep from clutching his head.

The rules to Tom's game had been very simple. She was not to use her hands until he allowed it. Lila hadn't asked what the punishment might be, but she was finding it increasingly difficult to keep her word as he inched his way down her body.

After caressing her breasts, Tom slid his tongue down to her stomach. Pressing gentle kisses along the slope of her hip, he moved to the curve of her thigh. His every touch was a fire of sensation. Lila moaned, shifting her hips beneath his kiss. She was on fire, and it was obvious he knew it.

As if he could no longer wait, Tom parted her thighs and dipped his head to the spot where she ached most for his touch. He smoothed apart the soft tangle of her hair to expose her completely to his every motion. As he stroked her with his tongue, Lila jumped beneath his touch.

"Tom!" She forgot her promise and wrapped her fingers in the lush darkness of his hair. Nothing mattered except his tongue and fingers working their magic upon her.

His lips suckled her as he had her nipples. Exquisite pleasure rocketed through her. The world faded away to mere blurs of red and black as she raised her hips to his mouth. The pleasure grew stronger and stronger, moving ever inward. The tight ball of her impending orgasm folded, tighter and tighter, in upon itself in every nuance of ecstasy as Tom continued making love to her with his mouth.

Tom slid his hands beneath her buttocks, and the heat of his fingers brought another delicious torture to her flesh. Pulling her closer to him, he moved his mouth away from her burning center. Though she whimpered, he merely blew a soft gust of cool air across her. Her thighs quivered.

Lila was poised on the edge of an incredible, tremendous orgasm. Aching with sensation, her entire body trembled. Tom puffed again, the air caressing her so delicately she would not have felt it had she not been so incredibly aroused. She wanted—no, needed—his lips and tongue on her again, but something held her back. She wanted to beg, but could not.

"Lila." The thrum of his whisper nearly sent her over the edge. "Open your eyes and look at me."

She couldn't look at him; she just could not. Not when he had reduced her to such a quivering bundle of nerves. Lila moaned lightly, her fingers kneading the sheet.

"Lila."

Lila opened her eyes. His hazel gaze didn't flicker as he met hers. Suddenly, it didn't matter to Lila if her voice cracked with desire when she spoke. Shame had no place in their lovemaking, nor did embarrassment. Nothing they did together could harm either one of them. All they shared was pleasure, nothing more. And if it gave him pleasure to have her speak, then she would do it.

"Yes, Tom," she murmured. "Please."

With a groan, he dipped his head back between her thighs. One kiss, then another, and she was undone. The tight ball of sensation that had been growing within her could no longer hold together. It shattered, driving a cry of sheer ecstasy from her throat.

She cried his name again, and he pulled her on top of him, unmindful of the stickiness left over from the caramel. She slid onto his length like he was coated in oil and cried out again from the sheer pleasure of him filling her. Tom rested his hands on her hips, but Lila needed no guidance. She rocked with him, moved in the rhythm they both set.

She could see nearly every inch of him as he lay beneath her. Now it was Tom's turn to close his eyes, and Lila liked watching him that way. His jaw was set fiercely in his arousal. The cords of muscle on his arms stood out as he clutched her hips nearly hard enough to hurt. The smooth ripples of his stomach rolled with each thrust of his hips.

"You feel so good." He opened his eyes. "I love making love to you."

Tom slipped one hand around between them so his thumb could press against her where she needed it most. She was going to climax again. Their rocking sped up. Wanting at the last moment to feel his lips against hers, Lila bent forward to crush her mouth to Tom's. He moaned inside her mouth as his thrusts became ragged with the force of his passion.

The tingling ecstasy burst through her again just as Tom shuddered beneath her and cried her name over and over. She could feel him throbbing inside her, the sensation sending another, final inferno of feeling through her. Then she collapsed on him as his hands curved around her back to hold her close.

"Wow," Tom said a few minutes later when Lila had rolled off him to snuggle against his side.

Lila laughed. "My thoughts exactly."

"I don't think this is what your sister had in mind when she wanted us to work together on the food."

"You don't know my sister." Lila ran a finger down his side. "She'd probably be more excited than I am about this."

He tipped her face until she was forced to meet his eyes. "Are you excited about this?"

Though he tried to shield his expression, Lila still saw the uncertainty lingering in his eyes. It touched her. She knew and understood her reasons for fear because William had certainly given her reason to be wary of handsome men. That Tom might be as uncertain of her was a surprise, but a poignant one.

She reached her mouth up to press a gentle kiss to his. "Tom, you are the best thing that's happened to me in a very long time."

He didn't answer her. Instead, he drew her close to him again and pressed his face into her hair. His silence didn't bother Lila. His actions had meant more than words could ever have.

Tom woke to the sound of the shower running. Even before he opened his eyes, he knew where he was. Lila's bed. Her scent, like fresh flowers and baby powder mingled with caramel, lingered on everything.

He stretched a little, and the sheet stuck to his leg. More caramel. Tom tossed the covers back and saw in the light of morning just what damage he'd done to her linens. The delicate flowered pattern was spotted disastrously with gooey caramel and bits of maraschino cherry.

From the doorway, Lila gave him a stern look. "I hope

you're satisfied." She wore the largest, most shapeless robe he'd ever seen, and an equally bulky towel completely covered her hair. She looked captivating. "Those were my very best Laura Ashley sheets."

He grinned, unable to help himself. "I'll wash them."

With a cry of mock fury, Lila launched herself across the room at him. Thankfully, the huge expanse of terrycloth surrounding her cushioned her landing. She pummeled his bare chest, laughed and met his mouth for a kiss. "You'll wash them. You'll get every last speck of caramel off those sheets, or I'll...."

"You'll what?" He pinned down her flailing hands. "Spank me?"

Lila laughed again, relaxing against him. "You'd love that."

"Maybe."

She felt so good, lying on him the way she was. Not even, Tom noted with small surprise, in a sexual way. Not that her kiss hadn't caused him to stir, but she just felt nice when she was near him.

"Penny for your thoughts. Fifty cents to act them out." Lila tickled his side.

"You seem so...comfortable." That was it. It seemed as though they'd been lovers for years. He sensed no awkwardness from her. More surprisingly, he felt none himself.

She looked seriously at him, her blue-ice eyes seeming almost violet in the morning light. "I don't do things half way, Tom."

"No, you don't." It was something he'd guessed about her right away. "You don't feel...weird? Having me in your bed, I mean."

She shook her head. The towel fell off and she didn't

replace it. Her tangled curls fell over her face, and she impatiently pushed them behind her ears.

"I don't feel awkward about having you in my bed because I invited you into it. I slept with you because I like you. Why would I feel awkward about seeing someone I like?" She appeared to think for a moment. "Is it awkward for you?"

He decided to be honest with her. "I don't usually stay over."

Her lovely brow furrowed. "Oh."

At once, he wanted her to see, as he did, what a good thing that was. "I never wanted to wake up next to any woman before."

She seemed pleased. "Oh!"

"I think I'd like to do it more often." Tom found himself saying things like that around her. Here, in her bed, with the bright morning light streaming in, it didn't seem like such a crazy thought.

Lila frowned slightly, pulling away. "Tom, it's too early in the morning to have this talk. You hardly know me."

"I know enough. I like the way you laugh. I like that you brought me flowers. I like that we can talk for hours. Isn't that enough?"

She picked fretfully at a thread on her robe. "It ought to be."

"It is."

Their conversation held such irony. In his experience, he had always said the things Lila was saying now. He understood her reluctance because he'd been there so many times himself.

Lila sighed. "I have fun with you. Even though we don't have anything in common—"

"You keep saying that." He took her hand away from her

robe and captured it with his.

"Because it's true."

Tom sighed and dropped her hand. "We have lots in common."

She quirked her brow at him, but granted him a smile. The grin, slight though it was, eased his mind.

"You drink coffee. I drink tea. You like westerns. I prefer horror. You like ham and cheese. I like matzo ball soup. You like running, and my idea of exercise is walking to the kitchen for a doughnut to go with my tea and my horror novel."

"Those are small things." Tom cupped her face in his hands and gazed into her eyes. "We both like to laugh. We both love our families. We both have jobs we love. Aren't those more important?"

Lila rested her head against his chest. Her hair was soft against his skin. Her cheek was smooth. He ran his fingers again and again through her curls and waited silently for her to speak. He'd had enough of these conversations before to know the timing was critical. He had made his decision about her, but that was worthless if she didn't feel the same. What she said next meant everything. Or nothing.

"I'm afraid."

Tom smiled. "Everyone's afraid."

She shook her head against him. "I dated a man two years ago. His name was William. He was very handsome, very charming. He was also incredibly arrogant, selfish, and cruel."

He knew where she was going with this, but kept silent. His looks had always been something he used or didn't use to get what he wanted. Now, for the first time, he wished he had not been blessed with his father's eyes and his mother's hair. Tom wished to be average.

Lila sighed. "You're not like that."

At her words, relief shot through him, making him realize just how certain he'd been she was going to tell him she didn't want to see him again. She met his gaze. "After he left me, he married a blonde with breasts the size of basketballs and a stomach you could probably bounce a quarter off of. He told me he didn't want to see me any more because he was done doing me a favor."

"Oh, Lila." He could see the pain in her eyes and wanted to smash the other guy's teeth in.

She blinked rapidly, clearing away a sheen of tears. Despite her obvious distress, her voice was strong. "He was a jerk. You're not."

"Lila, you're intelligent, funny and beautiful. Any guy who couldn't see that is more than a jerk. He's a moron."

She bit her lip and ducked her head before looking up at him again. "Thank you. I'm not beautiful, but thank you."

He'd been with plenty of skinny women who complained of being fat, gorgeous women who obsessed over tiny imperfections noticeable only to themselves, and women who downplayed their intelligence so they didn't intimidate the men they dated. He didn't get the impression Lila was fishing for compliments, or talking about bad qualities to emphasize the good.

He kissed her. "You're beautiful."

She blushed. "Stop."

"Do you really think that's what matters to me?"

She stared at him for a moment before replying. "I think you are used to being with a certain type of woman, Tom. And I'm not...I'm not that type of woman."

She sure wasn't. "But that's what I like about you."

Lila ran a hand along his arm, up to his shoulder, then tousled his hair. "That I'm not a sexpot?"

He kissed her hand. "I didn't say that."

Lila sighed and wriggled closer to him to put her head on his shoulder. Her voice was soft when she answered him. "One step at a time, Tom, okay?"

Another of his own lines come back to haunt him. "Okay."

Her breath heated his chest while her hand stole up to caress his bare skin. "You are the one who's beautiful, not me."

"Men can't be beautiful."

"Gorgeous then."

She traced the outline of his nipple with one fingertip. It stood erect at her touch. Tom put his hand over hers to stop her from moving more. He waited until she looked at him quizzically before speaking.

"Is that all I am to you, Lila?"

She licked her lips, then chewed lightly on the soft flesh. "At first."

"What about now?"

"I have a good time with you. A really good time."

He didn't want to push her further, not when she looked like she was about to run away at any moment. One step at a time, she'd said. He nodded.

"I have a good time with you, too."

She smiled and moved her hand again over his nipple. She bent to lick it, and the sensation of her hot, wet tongue on his flesh made his dick stir. She pushed him back on the bed and took him in her mouth, all the way to the base of his cock, so far down she could kiss his balls. When she did, he lifted his hips, and she backed off.

"Want me to stop?" she asked teasingly.

"Hell, no."

"Good."

She bent back to lick and suck him, and in just moments, he was like a teenage kid, ready to explode. He put a hand on her head. "Hold off. I don't want to come yet."

Lila sat up, her smile glistening. "That's something you don't usually hear."

"I want to make love to you first."

"Ah." The smile widened. "That's okay."

"But first I want to lick you."

Her smile faltered, but the heat in her eyes blazed. She swallowed and licked her lips again while she took a deep breath. At first he thought he'd made a mistake, that he'd frightened her again, but without another word, Lila straddled him, bent to kiss him, then slid her body up along his, until his mouth could reach her.

Tom put his hands on her hips and kissed her. She sighed when he did, and she trembled, but she didn't pull away. He slid his tongue along her folds and found the spot he knew brought her the most pleasure. She sighed again, louder this time. He cupped her buttocks as he licked her, and she tensed and relaxed as her hips began to move against his tongue.

Lila's head fell back, and her gorgeous brown curls fell down over her back to graze his knuckles. He wanted to tangle his hands in the silken tangle, but couldn't the way they were. He had to content himself with moving her body against his mouth and lips and tongue, with licking her until she began to moan, and until her body clenched in her first orgasm.

He wasn't done with her. Gently, Tom rolled her over while he slid open the nightstand drawer and pulled out a small foil packet. Sheathing himself quickly, because he could barely stand to wait, he slid inside her. Then he waited for a minute to catch his breath. Resting on his forearms, he leaned down to kiss her lips and cheeks while she smiled and wiggled beneath him.

"Stay still," he whispered.

"I can't," she whispered back with a giggle. She moved again, arching her back and tilting her pelvis to take more of him in.

"You have to," he replied. "Or else I'm going to be finished before we start."

She laughed again, a low, husky sound that made his balls tighten. "That's something I like about you. Most guys would not admit to a lack of control in the bed."

"I'm not admitting anything," he told her with a gentle thrust that made her moan aloud.

She grabbed his hips and pulled him closer to her. "Tom...less talking. More action."

"Your wish is my command," he whispered and kissed her again.

He'd said the words as a joke, light-hearted humor, but as soon as they left his mouth, he knew he meant them. He wanted to please Lila, not just in bed, but everywhere. He wanted to make her smile, hear her laugh. He wanted to take care of her.

Love her.

The thought filled his mind before he could stop it, but then the passion overtook him and he moved with her until he couldn't think any more.

Lila was late to work and didn't care. She had a pile of mail to go through and a crisis with the printer, and she didn't care about that either. Life is good, Lila reflected as she settled down at her desk. She felt like singing.

"*You* are late!" Darren announced from the doorway.

"I know." She grinned uncontrollably.

Darren looked at her carefully, then shut the door behind him and slid into the chair across from her. "Fess up, honey. You've got happy written all over your face."

"Let's just say I had an interesting evening."

Darren used his wonderful power of expression to let her know he wasn't fooled. "And morning, too, it looks like."

She shrugged, unable to stop smiling. "Maybe."

"Maybe, nothing!" Darren hooted, slapping the desk. "You got yourself a boyfriend!"

Lila shushed him and winced. "Why not take a memo and copy the whole company, Darren!"

Her assistant laughed and propped his feet up on the desk. "We won't need a memo. You can't hide your face, honey. You're in love."

She blushed and began sorting through her mail. Darren did have a disconcerting way of digging right to the heart of any matter. Not that she was in love with Tom. It was too soon. Wasn't it?

"I wouldn't say that." She struggled for coolness, but the smile kept creeping up on her mouth. Finally, she tossed the mail aside and let out a restrained whoop while twirling around in her chair. "Maybe."

Darren crossed his arms in front of him like a drill sergeant. "Spill your guts. I want to know everything."

Lila didn't have to think about what to say. The words tumbled out of her in a rush. "His name is Tom Caine. He owns The Foxfire. We met at my sister's showing a few weeks ago. That's it."

Darren snorted. "If that's it, I'm the Queen of Sheba. I know you better than that."

"He's...handsome."

Darren's brows lifted, and his feet came down off the desk with a thump. "Oh, no."

Lila groaned and buried her face in her arms on top of the desk. "He's gorgeous."

"But he's short, right?"

"No. He's at least six-two."

"Dumb?"

Again, she groaned. "Absolutely not."

Darren forced her to sit up and look at him. "The man is tall, gorgeous, and smart?"

She nodded. Her assistant let out another whoop, got up from the chair, and began doing his patented bump and grind around the desk. Lila, as always, couldn't help but dissolve into a fit of laughter.

"Girlfriend's back!" Darren slid back into the seat. "Lila, honey, I am so glad you have finally seen the light."

Lila put her hands on her hips and huffed. "Oh, come on. My social life hasn't been that bad."

Darren looked at her in such a way she had no doubts that he thought otherwise. "Since Bill the Bozo, Lila, all you've dated is computer geeks and mama's boys. I am serious."

He was right, of course. Other than Rivka, Darren was the only person Lila had told about William. Darren was also the only person who'd seen any of the men she'd gone out with since then.

"All those nights I helped you get ready?" He referred to the times she'd asked him to help her with her hair or makeup before a date. "I was wasting my time and my mascara. None of those men were good enough for you."

That sobered her. "Don't say that. Nobody isn't good enough for anybody."

Despite her cryptic response, she was sure Darren knew

what she meant. William had told her she wasn't good enough. Lila had vowed vehemently to never say the same about anyone else.

Her assistant looked chastened. "Sorry. But it's true."

Lila glanced back to the pile of mail now strewn in an untidy heap across her desk. Nothing could have put a damper on her day, but the pile of work she had to do was a good start. She began sorting the letters.

Darren picked up a few that had slid to the floor, then took the rest from her. "I'll do this. You have to meet with Corporate Carl in about fifteen minutes."

"Fifteen minutes!" Lila was aghast. She had forgotten about her planning meeting with Carl Houser, the president of Lymen Media. He wanted to discuss where her magazines were heading, an ominous question she wasn't sure she wanted to answer. Now she only had fifteen minutes to prepare.

"Love does make a person all mush-brained." Darren ducked out of the way before she could slap him. "Relax, Lila, it's only Corporate Carl. Just hike your skirt up a little and bat those pretty lashes."

That the company president was a known lecher did nothing to extend her confidence. She still needed to come up with justification for the way her four titles were doing in the marketplace. She began digging somewhat frantically for the sheaf of notes she had prepared.

"I don't even have anything to do with his stupid planning meeting." Lila ran her fingers through her hair in frustration. "It's all editorial and marketing! I'm just in charge of getting the stupid things out, for Pete's sake!"

She found the notes exactly where she'd left them. Skimming them, she was relieved to find her reports still made sense. She breathed deeply, finally allowing herself to relax.

Darren watched her solemnly. "I've never seen you this flustered. Whatever Mr. Gorgeous did to you last night must not have worn off yet."

She cast him an evil glare. "Darren, I'm not paying you to comment on my love life."

He shrugged. "No, honey, 'cause if you were—"

"I know. I couldn't afford your salary."

Darren grinned. "Am I going to meet this mystery man or what?"

"He'll be at Rivka's opening." Lila still wasn't sure she looked forward to that little shindig. "It's going to be a costume party, Darren. Want to come?"

He paused in the doorway. "Are you kidding me? A chance to see that crazy sister of yours, meet your new boyfriend, and party hearty all in drag? I wouldn't miss it for the world, honey!"

"Something told me you'd like the idea." Lila grinned.

"Don't worry, Lila. I'll let you know exactly what I think of him."

Lila gathered her notes. The question wasn't what Darren might think of Tom. It was what Tom might think of Darren. The thought made her laugh out loud. Still laughing, she left the office to go to her meeting.

The meeting didn't take long, thank heavens. Carl was brief and to the point. Archery Hunter magazine was the only one of her four titles that was actually doing well. Doll Collector, Early American Crafts, and British Life were all barely breaking even.

Hiding her apprehension, Lila presented her carefully planned reports showing that the fault lay in marketing and advertising, not with production. To her relief and surprise, Carl had emphatically agreed with her and even commended her on her performance under such circumstances and hinted at the prospect of a raise.

Consequently, the high Lila had been on since waking up in Tom's arms got even higher. Almost whistling, she swung by the mail room to drop off a few things before heading back to her office. She planned to take Darren to a nice, long, expensive lunch.

"Hi, Lila!" The eager voice shot out from behind the tall row of shelves that served as mail slots.

Lila's good mood dropped a notch. "Hey, Ned. How are you?"

"I'm just dandy." Ned Namey ogled her through one of the slots. "And how 'bout yourself, pretty lady?"

Lila repressed a grimace. "Oh, you know. Busy, busy."

Ned stepped out from his mailroom domain and hitched his pants up past his waist. He had really outdone himself this time. Kelly green linen pants, inadequately held up with a brown leather braided belt. Faded pink Izod polo shirt, collar standing up to brush his ears. Black loafers with tassels. He'd even added a watch today.

"Do you like it?" He must have seen her noticing it. "It's a Bolex."

"A Bolex?"

"Yeah, you know." Ned gave her a conspiratorial glance. "It's like a Rolex, but it's a Bolex. I got in New York when I went to the National Mail Handlers Convention."

"It's...really...nice." Lila mustered as much enthusiasm as she could. She handed him the pile of envelopes she needed to send out. "Here you go, Ned. Thanks a lot."

"So, when are we going to go out again?" Ned took the pile and began nonchalantly tossing each letter into its appropriate slot. "We had such a great time the last time."

"Boy, we sure did." Lila wished the floor would open up and swallow her whole. Or better yet, swallow Ned. "But...."

Ned suddenly turned from his letter sorting—the smarmy smile wiped clean from his face. It had been replaced by an expression of intense sincerity. Lila stifled a groan.

"I tried calling you a couple of times, but you didn't get back to me."

What could she say to that? She didn't have the heart to tell him the truth—that the one time she had agreed to go out with him had been a mistake. She'd gotten his messages, but had wimpily forgone returning his calls. She had hoped he'd get the hint.

"Sorry," she said. "I've just been...."

"Busy, I know."

"I'm really sorry," she repeated. "I don't know what else to say."

"You could say you'll go out with me again," Ned said in the hopeless voice of a man who expects to be shot down.

"Oh, I wish I could. I really do." Lila gritted her teeth. "But I've just started seeing someone."

"Oh."

She would rather have had someone hit her on the head with a frying pan than have to look at Ned's face. Lila felt terrible. Ned was nice. He was just too...well...Ned.

"I sure did have fun with you, though." Lila struggled to sound sincere. "Bowling, the stuffed-animal exhibit at the state museum. A lot of fun."

"Lila, you don't have to patronize me," Ned said with a nerd's quiet dignity. "I know you didn't want to go out with me again. It's okay. A woman like you never wants to go out with a man like me."

The similarity to her own words to Tom made Lila step back. "Oh, Ned."

"No, Lila, really, it's fine. I'm used to this. I just thought. ..." Ned trailed off for a moment, sounding wistful. "I just thought you were different. You're always so nice to me."

Oh, brother, Lila thought. How to respond to that? She couldn't tell him that she was just being nice to be nice, not being nice to be...well...nice.

"Ned, I'm sorry." It was the third time. "I really am seeing someone now, or else I'd love to go out with you again."

"I said you don't have to patronize me!" Ned snapped loudly. Two bright spots of color had appeared in his pasty cheeks. "I'm not much to look at, I know, but I'm not dumb!"

Lila's heart sunk into her stomach. Now she really didn't know what to say. Anything she could come up with would just make matters worse. "Ned..."

"Just go." Ned's voice rang with coldness, and he ducked back into his sanctuary. "I'll see you around. Good luck with your new boyfriend."

He sneered the last word before he turned his back on her and started again to sort the mail. Lila left the mailroom and hurried to get back to her office before she started to cry. She felt terrible about what had just happened, and the fact she was now on the other side of the table did not escape her. Was this how Tom had felt when she had said almost the same thing to him?

Darren took one look when she entered the office and shut the door. "Does this mean we're not going to lunch?"

Lila slumped into her chair and rubbed her temples.

Darren's words finally registered and she looked up. "No. Why?"

Her assistant frowned and pulled up the other office chair. She had never seen him look so serious. He looked worried.

"Corporate Carl really let you have it, huh?" He sounded sympathetic. "We going to be out of jobs, honey? 'Cause I got a great lead over at Caldwell Publications. My cousin's girlfriend's sister's niece works in human resources over there."

Lila stared at him blankly for a long moment before she realized he thought her glum mood was because of the planning meeting she'd had. "Relax, Darren, our jobs are safe. We might even be getting raises."

There was his excellent use of expression to convey emotion again. Both brows raised and his lips pursed, Darren sat back in his chair. "Then why did you come in here looking like your dog just died?"

"I just had a rather disturbing conversation with Ned."

"Nerdy Ned?"

Lila nodded. She leaned back in her chair and eased muscles she had not noticed earlier were sore. The reasons for her aches and pains would have made her smile an hour ago, but now Ned's accusations cast a pall over the memory of Tom's lovemaking.

Darren snorted. "What did he want?"

"He wanted to know when we'd be going out again."

Darren began to laugh in his wonderfully unrestrained way. At least she usually thought it was wonderful. Now she winced as his laughter filled the small office and probably carried out to the hallway despite the closed door.

"Darren! It's not funny!"

"Honey, I told you going out with him would be a mistake!"

She felt the beginnings of a headache. The morning's euphoria was completely destroyed. She felt just terrible about treating Ned so badly. "Keep your voice down, Darren! He's got feelings, too."

To her surprise, Darren quieted. "Lila, are you feeling guilty?"

"Maybe a little. I did just...blow him off."

"And telling him that you'd have more fun plucking your eyebrows with a pair of rusty tweezers than going out with him again—that would've been better?"

A smile twitched her lips. "I could've just told him up front that I thought he was very nice, but that I didn't think we'd ever be anything more than friends. Now I just hurt his feelings."

"Shoot, Lila, his feelings would have been hurt no matter what you told him. Face it, honey, 'there's someone for everybody' is just a myth."

"That doesn't make it right!" Guilt still assailed her. "He said something like women like me don't date guys like him."

"Well?" Darren looked clearly perplexed. "They don't!"

"But that doesn't make it right!" Lila rapped the desktop with her fist.

"Ah, I see." Darren shifted in his chair and propped his feet up on her desk. "This has got to do with Bill the Bozo, huh?"

It was nice to have a friend who knew your history. It saved a lot of explanation. She nodded, tearing off a used piece of paper from her notepad just so she'd have something to do with her hands while she talked.

"I made Ned feel the same way William made me feel." Repugnance filled her.

Darren clicked his tongue and shook his head. "William did it to you on purpose. You didn't set out to hurt Ned's feelings. There's a big, big difference, honey."

"I doubt if Ned would think so."

Her assistant sniffed. "So what you going to do? Date Ned just to make him feel better? To do him a favor?"

She winced at the force he put into his words. Darren knew the whole sad story of what had happened with William and how he had told her he'd been tired of doing her a favor. Darren was trying to provoke her.

"I feel terrible." She groaned, crumpling the note paper into a sweaty ball in her fist.

"What's this got to do with Mr. Gorgeous?" Darren took the paper away from her and tossed it into the trash.

Lila shrugged. "Nothing. Everything. I don't know. Nothing now, I guess."

"But before?"

"I told him when we met that men like him didn't date women like me." The confession made her feel stupid.

"What?" Darren yelled so loud Lila was grateful she had shut her door. "Damn, girl, what's the matter with you?"

He looked so righteously angry that Lila couldn't help smiling. "I'm a moron?"

"Yes, you are a moron. And I hope you get over that."

"I just don't want to get hurt again." Contemplating, Lila bit the end of her thumb. "And the way things are going, I think I could."

"Could, shmould." Darren sounded so much like Rivka, Lila had to smile. "You never get anywhere if you don't take risks."

"Do I pay you to give me advice?" Lila still felt horrible

about the scene with Ned, but Darren was right. William had hurt her on purpose. It didn't make what happened with Ned right, but it did make seem less wrong.

"You know what I got to say to that." Darren got up from his chair. "I thought we were going to lunch."

"Sure, let's go." She would carry the scene at the mailroom with her for a long time. Knowing she hadn't meant to cause Ned pain didn't make her feel any better about it, but at least it had made her think.

CHAPTER 6

Shoppers crammed the mall from one end to the next. Lila began to regret her decision to come at all. She hated being forced to press up against people she didn't know, and long lines at the cash register made her crazy. If she hadn't already scoured every specialty shop in downtown Harrisburg for the perfect gift to give her sister as congratulations on the gallery opening, she'd just turn right around and go home.

"Let's make a break for it!" Tom pointed to a spot in the crowd that had magically cleared.

For such a large man, he moved with the grace of a dancer. Grabbing Lila's hand, he wove them in and around the other shoppers until he had pulled her into the slightly less crowded food court. Spotting an empty table ahead, he dove for it and nearly knocked over a teenage couple more intent on seeing how many body parts they could press together than on watching where they were going.

"Sorry," Tom told the young man, who merely shrugged. "C'mon, Lila, let's sit down and have something to eat. I'm starved."

"My treat for putting you through all this."

"All what?" Tom looked around the crowded mall with mock surprise. "Being part of a stampede is my idea of a good time."

She laughed. She laughed a lot when she was with him. It was just the way he made her feel.

"Thanks for coming with me. I really want to find Rivka something special."

"Any reason to spend some time with you is good enough for me." Tom leaned over and brushed a kiss against her lips.

Lila knew she was grinning like an idiot, but couldn't help it. The past two weeks with Tom had been like something out of a movie. When work or other commitments prevented them from meeting for dinner, he invariably called her before going to bed. They'd spoken every day for two weeks and had never run out of things to talk about.

"What can I get you?" She wanted to kiss him again, but was well aware of the crowd around them. It wouldn't do to get carried away, and she knew herself too well. She didn't have a whole lot of self-control where Tom was concerned.

He wiggled his brows lasciviously. "You know what I like, baby."

Lila rolled her eyes. "Yeah, I know what you like. But what do you want me to buy you for lunch?"

"Cheeseburger, fries, soda. The heart-attack special."

"Hold down the fort. I see a couple of mall crawlers over there eyeing this seat."

"I'll guard it with my life." Tom spread out his hands as though to cover the entire table. "Hurry back. I'm so hungry I could eat a bowl of lard with a hair in it."

Lila screwed up her face in disgust. "You have such a way with words, Tom."

"Thanks."

"Modest, too."

Tom grinned an aw-shucks smile. "You've got me pegged, Lila."

She was pretty hungry herself. Shopping did that to her. She made her way through the throng, heading toward Mr. Burger. Though she tried to stay away from junk food, Tom's order had suddenly got her mouth watering. She gave the order to the paper-capped teen behind the counter, adding a chocolate milkshake instead of a cola for herself.

"In for a penny, in for a pound," she said wryly, mentally calculating the calorie load. "Or more like four or five pounds."

While she waited for the food, Lila glanced back to where Tom sat. He was no longer alone. A tall, auburn-haired woman now sat across from him. As Lila watched, the woman laughed, tossing back her head until her gorgeous hair flowed halfway down her back.

A tiny sense of unease crept into Lila's stomach. She shook it off. She bumped into people she knew all the time at the mall. Tom had obviously just met someone he knew.

And knew rather well. A sudden sick sensation flowed over her. The redhead leaned across the table to lay her hand across his. From Lila's angle she couldn't see Tom's reaction, but the other woman's face was clear as spring water. The redhead was smiling and fluttering her eyes. She was flirting.

"Order's up," the gangly youth in the Mr. Burger uniform announced.

"Thanks." Lila took the tray.

She didn't really want to walk back through the crowd. Not with the redhead still sitting in Lila's seat. Lila's mouth felt like sand, and the tray felt as heavy as stone.

She forced a blank smile to her lips and made herself put one foot in front of the other until she had reached the table.

"Lila!" Tom seemed glad to see her.

"Oh." The word came out from the other woman's painted lips in exaggerated innocence. "Am I sitting in your seat?"

"That's okay." It was a lie, but Lila set the tray down on the table and made room for it by pushing aside her own bag, though the redhead's purse was actually taking up more space.

"I was just leaving anyway." The other woman's tone clearly implied her haste to exit was mostly because of Lila's arrival. "I just saw Tommy here and had to stop and say hi."

Lila nodded silently, a look of what she hoped was neutral interest upon her face. The redhead got up, obviously reluctant to leave Tom's side though she'd already said she was going. Lila decided not to wait for the other woman to move away from the chair and instead made room for herself at the other end of the table.

"Lila, this is Heidi." Even with Tom's introduction, Heidi continued to hover over him. "We used to live in the same building before I bought my house."

"Which you've never invited me to see." Heidi pouted prettily.

Tom cleared his throat and looked from Heidi to Lila and back. "Sometime, Heidi, I promise."

"All right." Heidi sighed and squeezed his shoulder in a way that made Lila grit her teeth. "But you promised. You heard him, didn't you, Lila?"

"I certainly did." Even to herself, her voice sounded faint.

"See? Lila's my witness," Heidi said. "Well, Tommy, I've

got to run. It was great seeing you again. Call me...my number's the same!"

With a swirl of auburn hair, Heidi slipped off into the crowd. Lila kept her eyes fixed on the tray she was unloading. She refused to look at Tom. She wasn't going to make a scene, though the other woman had obviously been flirting.

"This burger looks great!" Tom enthusiastically tore open the grease-stained paper. "Thanks."

"No problem." She forced the lightness.

She nibbled her burger, though it sank like a stone into her stomach. Seeing Tom with the gorgeous Heidi hadn't done a lot for her appetite. It was too bad, too, because the burger really did look great.

"I haven't seen Heidi since I moved into my house." He sounded too casual. He washed down a handful of fries with some of his soda.

"Hmm."

"I hardly even know her."

Now she met his gaze. "You don't have to apologize for talking to someone else, even if she could be a supermodel."

"Her? No way. She couldn't model with a paper bag on her head."

His exaggerated comment brought a small smile to her lips. "Tom, I'm not blind. She was gorgeous."

Tom shook his head and grimaced. "She's got a big butt. Huge, in fact. And her left earlobe was bigger than the other one. Disgusting. I could hardly stand to look at her. She's a hag, a troll. She's a troglodyte, Lila." He shuddered.

Lila's smile turned to a laugh. "You have such a way with words."

"That's me." He had no pretense of modesty. "Mr. Eloquent."

"She called you Tommy." The fact no longer bothered

her.

Tom made a strangled noise in his throat. "Reason enough to despise her. Lila, she came over to me. I didn't ask her to sit down."

"It doesn't matter." It really didn't. "I don't own you. We've only been seeing each other a short time. We haven't even agreed not to see other people."

"Do you want to see other people?"

Their food lay uneaten while Lila thought about what to say. Her next words could be a big deal. "No."

He let out a sigh of relief. "Me neither."

"Don't rush into this—"

He stopped her with a kiss. "I'm not rushing into anything. If something's worth doing, it's worth doing right. And you, my lovely Ms. Lazin, are definitely worth doing."

A thrill shot through her at his innuendo. "You're bad, you know that?"

"But it's a good kind of bad." He winked.

They just sat there for a moment longer and stared at each other. The silly grin plastered on his face was a mirror of hers, Lila was sure. Suddenly, the mall didn't seem crowded at all. Suddenly, the only person she could see was Tom.

Tom was glad they had finished. By the time they'd eaten lunch, found a present for Rivka, and started making their way out of the mall, the crowds had grown even larger. Getting out at last was a relief, though being forced into such close proximity with Lila had its advantages. For one thing, he'd been able to link his fingers with hers at the merest excuse.

"Thanks again for coming with me, Tom."

They'd finally managed to escape the hordes of shoppers. They had just broken out of the building and had paused on the sidewalk to breathe in air untainted by the sweat of bargain-hunters.

"My pleasure."

It had been, too. Though he hated shopping, especially in the frou-frou, delicate sorts of shops she'd dragged him into, being with Lila made even porcelain clowns seem bearable. Not that she'd bought a porcelain clown, of course, and thank God. As much as he liked her, seeing her plunk down good money for such an atrocity might have dimmed his estimation of her.

She'd bought Rivka a delicate six-pointed star of stained glass. In vivid shades of purple, red, green, and blue, the star would look beautiful in the front gallery window surrounded by the hues of Rivka's paintings. It was a perfect choice, one that had made him think Rivka wasn't the only sister with artistic talent.

"Oh, no," Lila protested when he voiced his thought aloud. "I don't have an artistic cell in my body. I'm the pragmatic Lazin daughter. It's like that old joke about sisters, you know? She's the pretty one, and I'm the smart one."

"Does that mean poor Rivka's ugly and stupid?" He liked to see her blush at his teasing.

She immediately caught his meaning, which pleased him inordinately. He'd never been with a woman who didn't need his jokes explained to her. She didn't protest, which pleased him even more. He reached out to brush a stray chocolate curl from her cheek. He'd tell a thousand jokes if it made Lila smile. A light snow had begun to fall, the first of the season. It dusted the ground everywhere with white, like the sugar on a powdered doughnut. It made him feel like a kid. As they walked to where he'd parked his truck, he even managed to skid a little, sliding sideways through the slush like he was on a skateboard.

"Snow." Lila's face had lit up in wonder. "How pretty."

She tilted her head back to catch a flake on her tongue. At the sight of the small pink ribbon sticking out from between her perfect lips, the low flame of desire in his belly kindled into something stronger. Lila was giggling, trying without success to catch some snow. In the harsh fluorescent light from the parking lot, her face was sculpted into lines and shadows broken by the curve of her mouth as she laughed. She was beautiful.

"Tom? My God, is that you?"

The feminine voice from behind them broke him from his silent admiration of Lila's face. Her cheeks pinking, Lila stopped trying to catch a flake. Tom turned.

"Susan." He wasn't at all thrilled.

Cloaked with the reek of cigarette smoke, Susan exclaimed loudly in her husky voice how glad she was to see him. It had been ages, just ages, hadn't it? Why hadn't he called?

"And who's this?" Susan turned her bright, ferrety gaze on Lila and stuck out her hand. "I'm Susan Warner. A friend of Tom's."

"Lila Lazin." To her credit, Lila shook the other woman's hand with no apparent attempt to crush her fingers.

With the introductions over, Susan quite conspicuously looked Lila over from head to toe. Then, obviously dismissing her as no threat, Susan turned her attention back to Tom. She forced a hug on him, one he did his best not to return.

"Remember the time we went on that ski trip? What a

blast! Let's do it again this year, Tom! The ski club's having the same trip. Lila, do you ski?"

Lila looked like a rabbit flushed out in front of the lawnmower. "No, I don't."

"Too bad," Susan crooned, turning back to Tom. "Let me know, Tom, okay? You have the number."

Before he could stop her, she'd forced her lips against his cheek. Tom wasn't one to be rude, but he wanted to push the annoying woman away. Of all the times to run into her, just after meeting Heidi...it was a nightmare.

Then, thankfully, she was gone. The stench of her cigarettes still lingered, though. He saw Lila tactfully waving away the air in front of her nose, as if to disperse the foul odor.

"We belong to the same ski club," he began by way of explanation.

Lila held up a hand to stop him. "Tom, it's okay. Really. You had a life before I came along. I understand that."

"I just don't want you to think I dated all those women." In fact, he'd dated both of them once or twice, which was one or two times too many in his opinion.

"All those women?" Lila quirked her brow at him. She was giving him "the look." He was coming to realize it meant she wasn't up to taking any bull. "I only counted two."

"Two in the same day." He suspected that little fact hadn't slipped by her.

"You dated women, so what?" She shrugged, though the effort seemed forced. "I'd have been surprised if you hadn't."

"Because of the way I look." It angered him it had come back to that again. He finally unlocked the doors to the Tahoe using the remote entry. He doubted he'd have been able to find the keyhole with the way his fingers had become numb. His whole body, in fact, was becoming numb, a feeling he was not used to and definitely did not like.

Lila gave a simple reply. "Yes. You can't run away from the fact that you're gorgeous, Tom. Not any more than I can pretend to be anything more than average. It's the way we're made."

"It's not!" he shouted, suddenly angrier than he'd ever been. "You're not average, Lila! Not to me!"

Lila, concern clear in her blue-ice eyes, reached out to cup his cheek. He leaned into her touch and covered her hand with his own. He kissed her fingers.

"You're beautiful to me. I've never felt so comfortable with anyone before. A thousand women could come on to me and I wouldn't even look at them twice. I love the way you look, the way you smell, the sound of your voice. I love everything about you."

His speech had left him breathless. Lila looked stricken, not the way he wanted her to look at all. Tom kissed her, and she let him. At least she didn't pull away.

"Be careful what you say," she murmured against his chest.

He thought he heard the threat of tears in her voice, and the thought he might have made her cry stung him like a blow.

"Words can be powerful, Tom."

"I meant everything I said."

She took a deep, trembling breath and shivered. Tears glistened in her eyes. As he watched, one crystal droplet slid down her cheek. He wiped it away.

"Don't...." She paused as if to gather courage. "Don't say it if you're not sure."

He hadn't been sure when he'd blurted the words, but somehow, seeing her single tear had made him certain now.

"I'm sure. I love you, Lila."

She let out a tiny cry, half laugh and half sob. "You hardly know me!"

"How well do you have to know someone who feels so much like part of yourself?" His tone was quiet.

The snow fell faster and covered her hair with lacy flakes. She looked as though she wore a veil. A wedding veil.

"Those women—"

"Sharks." The word was blunt. "Sharks who feed on bachelors. Any eligible guy with a decent job is up for grabs to them, and they just circle and circle until they snag one."

Lila twisted her mouth. "That's somewhat chauvinistic of you. Not all women are like that. I'm not, and I've never been married."

He was glad to see the tears had faded. "You're smart. You know who you are, and that's what I like about you. You don't need a man to define who you are."

She looked doubtful. "You make me sound like some rampant feminist career old maid."

Her fingers toyed with the ends of his scarf. Tom liked that she felt comfortable enough with him, even now, to touch him so casually. He laced his fingers with hers as best he could through the mutual bulk of their gloves.

"Because I'm not." She might be allowing him to hold her hands, but her voice was still all thorns and no rose. "I'd like to get married someday, Tom. Have a family, all that."

"Good."

Lila's creamy cheeks flushed. "I just meant—"

"You're no shark. They are, and you're not."

Lila smiled mischievously. "They were both rather predatory."

Tom rolled his eyes. "You don't have to tell me."

She peered at him through the snow fringing her lashes.

"I'm sure it's not as nice as it might seem. Being chased like that, I mean."

He noticed her shivering. The air had become much colder, and the snow was coming down faster. "Let's get inside."

Tom helped Lila into the Tahoe, then climbed in. She was right. Having women throw themselves at him had seemed great for a while, but had lost its luster lately. "When someone likes me or dislikes me because of the way I look...." Tom voiced aloud for the first time thoughts he had barely realized he had. "I can't really care about how they feel. Their opinion of me isn't real."

Lila bit her lip and appeared to think. "At least my relationships have been with people who like me. Really like me, I mean."

Except for William, he knew she was thinking, but didn't say. Again, he wanted to find the jerk and throttle him.

"I was a lonely guy before you came along." He wanted to lighten the mood that had suddenly grown too serious. "I was shark bait."

Lila gave him the look again. "That you are incredibly handsome helped, I'm sure."

"The only person I want to think I'm handsome is you." He pretended to think. "And maybe my mother."

"Well good luck, sweetheart." Lila laughed. "I think you're out of luck there."

Tom grinned. "Then you'll just have to stay with me all the time so you can help me fend off all those man-hungry women."

"Maybe we can get you one of those cages like on Underwater Kingdom."

She linked her fingers with his. He suddenly noticed

how cold the air in the truck had turned with the snow coming down so quickly. The roads were going to be dangerous if they didn't leave soon.

"I'm sorry it bothers you so much." He buckled his seatbelt and heard her buckle hers.

Once again, Lila didn't need to ask him to explain himself. He saw by the way her fingers played restlessly with her seatbelt that she knew exactly what he meant.

She sighed. "It does bother me. But I guess it's something I'll have to get used to."

"If I could change things, I would."

"Don't say that." In the green glow from the dashboard her eyes were luminously, eerily lovely. "Don't ever wish to change who you are. I like everything about you just the way it is."

It was only as he put the truck into gear and drove into the snow Tom realized one thing. She had said "like." He'd told her he loved her, and Lila hadn't said it back.

In her own bed, sleep evaded Lila. She turned onto her side and grumbled when her nightgown tangled around her legs. The moment after she become comfortable in the new position, she suddenly felt too hot and had to toss off the covers. Moments after that, of course, she got the chills and had to wrestle the comforter back on.

It was because she was alone. The bed seemed too big and too empty. She missed Tom.

"Damn."

He'd said he loved her, and like an idiot, she had said nothing in return. Love! Tom Caine had said he loved her, Lila Lazin.

She had no doubt he meant it. Though the physical time they had known each other was short, the emotional time was much longer. Two people couldn't talk for hours every night without learning something about each other.

But did she love him? What wasn't there to love? She'd already established that he was handsome. A successful businessman. Kind, generous, and compassionate. He had a wonderfully witty and weird sense of humor. That they had nothing in common didn't seem important any more; taste in soft drinks and reading material didn't count for much in the long run. What really mattered was how they connected.

But love? Lila had only been wildly in love once—with William. Though the thought made her cringe now, she had definitely loved the jerk. That he had been completely and totally unworthy of even her lowest affections she had no doubt now, but at the time he'd been like a gift from heaven.

If she could tell William Darcy she loved him, what in the world had held her back from telling Tom? Fear? Probably. Definitely. Love had a funny way of showing up when you least expected it. She wasn't afraid he was going to turn out to be another William. Nor was she afraid Tom was merely filling her head with pretty words to get her into bed.

She was afraid that what had happened in the mall would always happen. How could she stand up to that? Constantly standing aside while beautiful women made passes at Tom? Whether he responded or not, it didn't really matter. The sharks would keep circling as long as he was in the water.

She needed to talk to someone. It was well after midnight. Rivka would either be asleep or busy with Mick.

The last thing Lila wanted to do was interrupt either her sister's sleep...or other activities.

Instead, she dialed Darren's number. The phone rang twice before someone answered. She didn't recognize the voice.

"Darren?" she ventured anyway.

"This is Lance," the male voice on the line said. "Who's this?"

She heard herself stutter. "This...this is Lila."

"Boss lady!" Lance had a deep, rumbling voice that reminded Lila of a freight train. "Hang on, Lila, and I'll get him for you."

"Honey, what's wrong?" Darren asked.

"Nothing." Lila was suddenly embarrassed. What was she thinking, calling Darren so late? He had a life, too, one it sounded like she was interrupting.

"You don't call me at one a.m. to chat about the weather, honey. I know there's a blizzard outside and all, but that ain't exactly something I couldn't figure out myself."

"There's a blizzard?"

She had known it was snowing, but since she preferred sleeping in complete darkness, she'd drawn the blinds when she'd gone to bed. Now she sprung from beneath the covers and tugged up the window shade.

"That's what I said, honey. Me and Lance here were just lighting a fire and toasting some marshmallows."

"At this time of night?" Lila asked dubiously.

"Well, no one's going to work tomorrow, Lila." From the background came Lance's deep, rumbling laugh. "Weatherman said we're going to get four feet at least."

There was something so magical about a snow-covered world. The flakes were huge and soft, coating everything in a layer of white. She wished she could be sharing the snow and its magic with Tom, but they had agreed he wouldn't stay over on weeknights. Too many tired mornings could wreak havoc on both their careers.

"He told me he loved me." Once the words shot from her mouth, it was too late to take them back. Lila slammed the pillow and groaned.

"He said he loved her!" Darren's shout nearly burst her eardrum, and Lance whooped in the background. "Honey, I knew this guy was good for you!"

"I didn't say it back."

"Oh." Silence. Then, not to her, "She didn't say it back."

"Why not?" She heard Lance's fainter voice.

"You heard the man. I know, 'cause that voice carries, honey. Why didn't you tell Mr. Gorgeous the same thing?"

"I don't know." Lila sighed and scrubbed her face.

"All you've done for the past two weeks is eat, sleep, and breathe that man. I know, 'cause I've been up to my ears with all the things that keep slipping your mind. Not that I'm complaining, Lila, 'cause you know I'd do anything for you. Just remember this when raise time comes around, that's all."

"Have I been that bad?" Lila wriggled in embarrassment.

"Honey, I haven't seen anyone smile so much since the time my Aunt Nita spent the night with Lefty and Righty, the Samson twins."

"I don't think I want to hear the rest of that story." That was a picture she definitely did not want in her mental photo album. "Thanks anyway, Darren."

He laughed. "Lila, this guy isn't William Darcy."

"I know."

"So what's holding you back?" Darren paused. "Are you afraid?"

"I think so." Lila let the shade fall down and crawled back into bed. "He is different from William, Darren, and I think that's what I'm afraid of. That he won't leave me."

"Why is that a problem?"

She related all that had happened at the mall and how she'd felt. How watching women flirt with Tom day after day might wear her down. That even though he might not leave her, she might have to leave him because she couldn't face comparing herself to all those women.

"Do you think he's comparing you, Lila?"

"That's the thing." Lila twirled the phone cord. "He says no, and I believe him. He says he thinks I'm beautiful."

"But you don't think so."

Lila gave a flat reply. "Rivka is beautiful. The redhead at the mall is beautiful. The hostess at The Foxfire is beautiful."

"And so are you." She could just imagine his expression. "Lila, honey, you may not be RuPaul, but you've got all the right pieces in all the right places."

"Thanks, I think."

"It's not the color of your eyes or what's in your bra that made him fall for you. It's what's inside you, honey. And if you don't love what's in your own self, how can you love what's in anybody else's?"

"How do I know if I love him or not?" Lila waited for an answer.

Darren snorted. "What am I, your fairy godfather? You just know."

She sighed. "I really ought to start paying you more."

"Overtime, honey," Darren said. "Overtime."

CHAPTER 7

"WHAT AM I GOING TO DO?" Rivka shrieked so loudly Lila had to hold the phone away from her ear. "Everything's snowed in! My paintings are stuck someplace in Pittsburgh, Lila, and the opening's in three weeks!"

"Calm down." Lila tried to be as soothing as she could with Tom's tongue tracing erotic designs on her stomach. "We still have time."

"Time!" Rivka was really rolling now. "This damn snow will be here until Memorial Day!"

Lila stopped Tom's fingers just before they unbuttoned the last button of her blouse. It was difficult enough to think of ways to calm her frantic sister without him distracting her. Tom grinned as if he knew what she was thinking and mouthed, "Get off the phone."

"Lila, are you listening to me?" Rivka let out a wail. "This is a disaster!"

"Oh, Rivka." It was hard to be concerned about Rivka's histrionics when Lila herself felt so darned great. Having Tom come over on his cross-country skis had seemed like a crazy idea when he'd mentioned it before; now she was happy he'd been crazy enough to do it. "The price of kumquats, now that's a disaster. This snow is just a glitch."

Even Tom could hear Rivka's response. Wincing, Lila held the phone away from her ear. Tom laughed.

"Who's that with you?" Rivka paused. "Lila?"

"We've been caught," Lila whispered, punching him lightly. Then, to Rivka, "It's Tom."

For once, Lila was glad to hear she'd shocked her sister into silence. Tom began his quest to reach her underwear again. She pushed his hand away firmly. Tom didn't seem deterred.

"Tom Caine?"

"Yes." Lila giggled as the man-in-question's lips found a particularly ticklish spot. "The one and only."

"He's at your house."

"Yes, he's here to talk about...the menu for the gallery opening." Lila knew her sister wouldn't settle for that answer.

"How did he get there? There must be four feet of snow outside! Everything's shut down!"

"He...skied." Lila struggled not to laugh, though Tom had continued his ticklish quest.

"He skied?"

At least Rivka wasn't shrieking any more. This new tidbit of information about Lila's private life had temporarily distracted her from her own problems.

"Yes, on his cross-country skis." Lila was being deliberately obtuse.

"He skied through a blizzard to talk about menu options for my opening." Rivka's voice clearly stated she didn't even believe it herself.

"And some other things." Lila couldn't resist teasing her sister. Actually, she was happy Rivka had discovered the truth about Tom. Her sister, while overbearing, would be ecstatic for her.

"Lila-love." Rivka's voice was filled with admiration. "Is there something you should be telling your big sister?"

Tom grabbed the phone away from Lila, playfully holding it up so high she couldn't reach it. "Didn't your sister tell you she's in love with me?"

Lila couldn't hear Rivka's response. Her face had become an oven anyway. She hadn't told him yet herself, but she couldn't find it within herself to get angry at his audacity.

"Since your showing," Tom was saying. "Yeah, I thought so, too, but I won her over."

Then he was soothing Rivka in a way Lila never could. Somehow, he just knew all the right words to settle the artist's fears about her upcoming opening. Within five minutes, Tom had hung up the phone.

"I told her the food is completely under control." He pulled her into the crook of his arm. "I said we were planning on cooking all day."

"She knew you weren't referring to the kind of cooking one does in the kitchen, I presume." Lila snuggled in close.

"Of course."

They sat in comfortable silence for a time. The fire crackled, the sofa was soft, and the snow falling outside the picture window was soothing. Lila, who hadn't had much sleep the night before, began to doze in the warmth and serenity of Tom's embrace.

"You don't mind what I said to your sister, do you?"

Lila's heart thumped. "No."

"Because it seemed pretty presumptuous of me, after I thought about it. I mean, since I don't even know if it's true."

Now her heart thumped even more fiercely, and her palms began sweating a little. The fire, which had seemed pleasantly cozy before, now felt more like an inferno. She licked lips gone suddenly dry. "I love being with you."

Say it! her mind screamed. Nothing could be more perfect than this moment. The fire, the snow, every detail made for a romantic scene. Yet, somehow, the words wouldn't come.

"I love being with you." Tom linked his fingers through hers in a gesture so natural it made her smile. "But that's not necessarily the same thing, is it?"

"No."

They sat in silence for a few more moments, hands linked. Content to feel the thump of his heart against her cheek, Lila laid her head on his chest.

"I don't want to pressure you, Lila." Tom pressed a kiss to her temple. "I don't want to do that at all."

She twisted to look up at him. The sun was too bright for the firelight to be anything more than a hint reflected in his gorgeous hazel eyes. In any light, though, he was still the handsomest man she'd ever seen. His looks no longer bothered her.

"You're not. I've been thinking a lot, since last night."

He brushed his fingers through her hair. "Good things, I hope."

"Very good." At once, it seemed very important that she reach up to kiss him. Lila pressed her lips first to his forehead, then each of his eyes, and finally his mouth. She lingered there for a long moment, feeling the softness of his lips beneath hers. The kiss was sweet, gentle, but with the undertone of desire she had come to recognize so well. And yet, when it came right down to saying what she needed to... she couldn't.

Fear froze her tongue and closed her throat. She wanted to tell him she loved him, but the memory of William's face kept her from speaking. Instead, she kissed him again.

"What was that for?" His tone was pleased.

"Because you're a big goofball."

Tom sat back on the sofa, arms behind his head and rolled his eyes. "Nice. Always dreamed of a woman calling me that. You've just made my dreams come true."

She tilted her head as she reached out to push away the long bangs from his eyes. "You're crazy, you know that?"

He captured her hand. "Crazy for you."

She moved forward and kissed his mouth, then pulled back enough to look into his compelling hazel eyes. "I think my furnace is on the blink. It's a little chilly in here. Any ideas about how I could get warmed up?"

Tom curled his arm around her neck. "I think I could arrange something."

"Another thing I like about you," Lila told him. "You're very resourceful."

He waggled his inky eyebrows at her, then quirked one and put on a fake, posh accent. "Indubitably."

That made her laugh. She put his hand on her breast and curled the fingers around her already taut nipple. "Let's get make out and watch old movies."

"Make out?" He looked like he was pretending to think. "With you? I don't know, Lila. That's awfully presumptuous of you."

She knew him well enough by now to have been prepared for a smartass reply, and she greeted it promptly with a pillow to the head. He ducked and yelped, then grabbed the pillow from her and threatened her with it. He didn't hit her, though, just held it up before tossing it unceremoniously to the floor and gathering her in his arms.

His tongue parted her lips and she giggled, then relaxed into his embrace. His mouth moved over hers with sweet perfection, fitting with her lips the same way he fit her body. Like they'd been made for each other.

"Lila."

She blinked. "Yes, Tom." He sighed and brushed a kiss along her cheek before finding her lips again. "You think I'm a big dork, don't you?"

"Of course not!" Shocked, she sat back and searched his face for signs he was joking again. "Are you serious?"

Tom only stared before nodding. "You expect me to be more...suave. Don't you?"

Actually, she found his lack of ego endearing and charming, as well as flattering. She shook her head. "No, Tom. I don't think you're a dork."

For the first time, she had a better appreciation of what being judged on his looks had done to him. "I think you're smart, and funny, and incredible in bed. I think you're kind and generous, and you make a great omelet. I most definitely do not think you are a dork."

He grinned. "How about when I do this?"

He made the stupidest face she'd ever seen on a man, but it made her laugh out loud. "Except when you do that."

He rearranged his features into a more normal expression. "Just checking."

He reached for the remote control and turned on a classic movie station. Then he pulled her onto his lap. "Didn't you say something about making out?"

She'd been joking, a little, but readily accepted his kiss. "Sure."

And make out they did. She hadn't kissed for so long at

a time without getting naked since...well, since high school. Back when a boy's hand on her breast was an advance to be gracefully fended off, rather than an expected pleasure.

Back then, hours of kissing on the rec room sofa had left her stomach a tight mess, her panties damp, her breasts aching for a release she didn't really understand. A lot had changed since high school. Now, though the affects on her body were the same, Lila knew exactly what she was missing.

Tom had pulled her legs over his lap, but though one strong hand moved back and forth from her thigh to her hip, he hadn't even made a move to touch her anyplace else. His entire concentration focused on her mouth, her lips and face, the curve of her neck, the lobes of her ears.

Lila slid her leg closer, over the hard bulge in his pants. Tom's breath caught in his throat, and he paused in kissing her to cup her face in his hands. She thought he would say something, but he didn't...just bent back to brush his mouth lightly on hers in a teasing kiss that made her groan in frustration.

"You're driving me crazy," he whispered.

Lila laughed. "Me? Driving you?"

Tom nodded, eyes bright. He ran his tongue across his full mouth, and Lila had no trouble imagining how it would feel on her skin. "Kissing you is...hard."

That made her frown and punch him. "Nice. Thanks."

"No. I mean, only kissing you is hard. I want to make love to you so bad."

She tilted her head to look at him, then ran her fingers down his cheek. "So what are you waiting for?"

"I don't know." His grin melted her further. "I don't want it to be over yet. I want to make love to you forever."

That was possibly the sexiest thing a man had ever said

to her, and her thighs clenched in a pre-orgasmic spasm so strong it rippled her entire body, and a low noise escaped her throat.

Her breath hitched. "Forever's a pretty long time, Tom."

In reply, he leaned forward and kissed her again. This time, he didn't tease. His tongue swept inside her lips, plunged deep, and he did with his mouth what she'd been longing for him to do with his penis. He made love to her with nips and licks and kisses, and the thrusts of his tongue echoed the clenching in her belly and thighs.

She was going to come, and he hadn't even touched any part of her body other than her face. Oh, she was going to come, now, and all he had to do was keep kissing her. If he touched her, she'd explode, go off like a rocket, all it would take was just the right pressure, the lightest touch, a breath.

Now she was on his lap, straddling his hips, her center pressed to the metal of his belt buckle and his hands holding tight to her butt. He bit her throat hard enough to make her gasp, but it didn't hurt, just it sent a spear of pleasure straight to her clitoris. She rocked against him. Her fingers tangled in his hair, and she pulled his head back so she could devour his mouth like he'd been devouring hers.

Even with the layers of clothing between them, Lila had no trouble feeling the throb of his penis against her. Tom lifted his hips to rub her further, until her orgasm quaked through her and sent her reeling into an abyss of ecstasy.

A minute later, when she could think again, Lila blinked and looked into Tom's heavy-lidded eyes. As with everything between them, Lila didn't get embarrassed at her passionate display. She sighed and snuggled close to him.

It wasn't until the field in front of her suddenly bloomed with flowers the size of her head that Lila awoke with a start. She'd been dreaming, which meant she'd been sleeping. Guiltily, she sat up, wincing at the stiffness in her legs from the awkward position. If she was sore, she couldn't imagine what Tom felt like.

"Sorry," she said. "I fell asleep."

"I didn't care." Tom shifted her weight so she no longer sat on his lap. "It was nice. Holding you like that. I can't feel my legs anymore, but it was nice."

"Oh, no!" she cried, chagrined. "Tom, you should've woken me up."

He grinned, and despite the recent sexual explosion, his smile sent a tingle of arousal through her. "Ah, who needs legs anyway? Mine are too long. Can't find pants to fit."

"You're such a goofball," Lila told him. Heat flared in her cheeks at the memory of what had passed between them. "How long was I out?"

"Maybe fifteen minutes or so. Not long."

More guilt poked her. "That was amazing."

Heat blazed in his gaze. "Yeah. It was."

Lila had never been with a man who gave pleasure without expecting immediate payback. She waited to see if Tom would gaze pointedly down at his still-bulging crotch, or even take her hand and put it on his erection. He didn't. And maybe, she thought with some amazement, he wasn't going to. Maybe he really was content to have given her an orgasm without demanding one for himself.

"You are so different than I expected," Lila told him, and was pleased to see his mouth quirk into a self-effacing grin.

"So you've forgiven me for being pretty?"

She took his hand. "Forgiven."

Tom kissed her, softly, with a promise of more to come. "Let's go to the restaurant."

"The Foxfire?" The change of subject confused her. "Why?"

"Because I'm starved, and I happen to know you don't have any food in the house. C'mon, Lila, we can walk there from here easily."

"We'll have to," Lila reminded. "The roads are closed."

"Even better. We'll be able to make snow angels in the street without fear." Tom grinned as he squeezed and kissed her again.

"I don't have any skis." Her protest was weak. Already she knew his enthusiasm was going to win her over, but she had to make a token effort. "There's a blizzard outside. Wouldn't you rather stay in here by the fire with me?"

Her wheedling had no affect on him. Tom was up and off the couch so suddenly he almost dumped her on the floor.

"Me need food." Tom grunted, cave-man style. He hopped up and down while thumping his chest fiercely. "Lila come with Tom for food!"

Lila got the giggles. He was acting ridiculous, but she didn't care. In fact, his total disregard for how silly he might look or sound only made her feel more comfortable with him.

"I have some ice cream left." She tried to be as seductive as she could, knowing her ploy to stay out of the cold wouldn't work.

"Ice cream not food! Me need man food, steak and potato!"

Lila groaned. "Tom, it's cold out there!"

"Lila." Tom mimicked her whining tone perfectly. "The walking will keep you warm."

"You'd rather walk a mile in the freezing blizzard than stay here with me?" she asked mock-sadly. "The magic's already gone."

She sighed, shaking her head. With a Neanderthal's

roar, Tom jumped on her and began pummeling her with the sofa cushion. Lila grabbed the nearest pillow she could find and tried in vain to defend herself.

In no time, Tom had pinned her arms to her sides. "Are you trying to make me feel guilty for wanting to eat instead of make love to you?"

"Yes." She tried to catch her breath after all the laughing.

"A relationship based on sex will never last, Lila." His eyes were a picture of wounded masculinity. "I can't tell you how it hurts me to hear you say you'd rather make love to me than feed me. How selfish of you, to put your own base, perverted needs before mine—"

He didn't have time to finish his sentence because Lila had shoved a cushion in his face. The pillow fight was on again—the two of them wrestling like children. Only when Lila threw a pillow at Tom, knocking over a lamp, did they both stop.

"You're pretty immature, Lila." Tom grinned. "But I like it."

Her stomach rumbled, and the exercise had heated her up enough that facing the cold didn't seem so daunting. "Now I'm hungry."

"Hungry enough to brave the weather outside?"

She looked out the window. "Yep. But I still don't have any skis."

"Got a cookie sheet?"

She frowned. "Yes, why?"

Tom just smiled. "You'll see."

⊐⊏

Behind him, Lila was letting out little gasps of hysterical

laughter. With every forward movement of his feet, she let out another stream of breathless giggles. She'd been laughing for fifteen minutes straight.

"You're going to pee your pants," he remarked over his shoulder.

More laughter. It had taken on a high-pitched, desperate quality. He glanced around to see Lila clutching the edge of the cookie sheet with one mittened hand and her stomach with the other.

"Stop!" She burst into another peal of laughter as he jerked forward on the ropes again. "It hurts! Oh, it hurts!"

Tom slid his next foot forward. "You think you hurt." The ropes he'd attached to his waist jerked again on the cookie sheet. "I'd like to see you tug me around on a cookie sheet."

Lila laughed harder. Suddenly, his load lightened so much he knew she had fallen off even before he heard the snow-muffled thump of her landing. Without the weight to hold him back, Tom shot forward too fast and lost his balance. He went arse over elbow into a pile of drifted snow; his skis tangled like taffy.

Thankfully, they'd reached the restaurant. It even looked like the snowplow had managed to get through the main street, so all he had to do was crawl another few yards and climb over the mountainous drift and he'd be all clear. For the moment, Tom was just content to lie in his crumpled heap and listen to Lila laugh.

"Tom, are you all right?"

Her nose and cheeks were red as raspberries, and her eyes shone with tears of laughter. Most of her hair was tucked up inside the ugliest ski cap he'd ever seen, but a few dark curls had managed to escape around her face. Snow covered her from hat to boots as she climbed to her feet. She looked so lovely he didn't even mind having to watch her from a pile of snow.

"Whose bright idea was this anyway?" he growled as he struggled to get to his feet. It was obvious he'd only be able to do that by kicking off his skis, so he did. Lila reached out and grasped his hand to help him up. He took her offered mitten, not because he thought she'd really be any help, but because he wanted to touch her.

"Yours." She showed no shame at all. "Totally yours, as I recall. I was completely content to stay in by the fire, but no! You had to traipse out into the wilderness in search of steak and potato."

"Lila." Tom held up his secret weapon. "You do realize I have a handful of snow, don't you?"

She shrieked and tried to run, but the snow was too deep. She only managed to tangle her feet and fall next to him in the drift. Her lips were like ice against his, but their kiss soon warmed them both. His tongue stroked the velvety inside of her mouth and she responded. They stayed there, kissing, long enough for his fingers to grow numb even through his heavy gloves.

"Think we can make it over this mountain?" Lila pointed at the massive mound of snow pushed up by the plow.

Tom tipped an imaginary hat at her. "Race you!"

The climbed over the top, slid down the other side, and landed right in front of the door to The Foxfire. Some civic-minded person had been along the sidewalk earlier with a snow blower. Though the blizzard had dumped several more inches since then, the way was at least clear enough for them to get inside.

"It's dark," Lila said. "And cold."

Tom could fix that, and he did. Leading her back to the

kitchen, he turned on the lights and lit the oven. Within minutes, the industrial size oven had warmed the room considerably.

"We need to get our clothes off." Lila shivered. "We're both soaked."

Tom pulled her closer for another kiss. "Sounds like a good idea to me."

Lila pushed him away gently. "We could've done that at my house, stallion. We came here to eat, remember?"

She began peeling off her layers of clothing, and for a moment, all Tom could do was watch. She tugged off her hat and set free the coiled masses of her hair. It tumbled around her face in wild disarray. She didn't even bother to comb through it, which he loved. He could think of any number of his female acquaintances who would have been mortified to be seen in such a state, but Lila didn't care.

Next came her bulky field coat and mittens, the two pairs of thick sweatpants and her sweatshirt. Finally, she wore only a thin set of insulated underwear that clung to her like plastic wrap. Her perfect breasts and hips were completely outlined by the thin fabric, and he swallowed heavily. What made the sight even more erotic was that Lila obviously had no idea about the way she looked. That, coupled with the fact his penis was still half-erect from all the foreplay earlier, made him take a step back to keep from charging over to her and ravishing her right there on the kitchen floor.

"C'mon, Tom. You're going to catch a chill."

He physically had to shake himself in order to clear himself of the spell he'd been under. She was right. Already he felt his sodden clothes making him shiver.

She watched him with the same intensity with which he'd watched her undress. Their eyes locked as he stripped down to his final layer, boxer briefs that did nothing to hide the way he was feeling at the moment. He hooked his thumbs in the waistband, but paused. Tom knew as well as any man the difference even one article of clothing could make. He didn't want to destroy the sensuality of the moment.

"Look at you." As if in a daze, she reached out to run her hand along the smooth curves of his chest. At her touch, his erection strained against the black fabric of his briefs, but he forced himself to remain still. Lila caressed his nipples and softly rolled them beneath her fingertips. She let both hands slide along the rippled flatness of his stomach and moved closer until he could feel her breath on his skin. Still, he didn't move.

Slowly, almost reverently, she traced the waistband of his briefs and dipped her fingertips slightly inside. His knees felt weak. She stared at him hungrily, taking what looked like an almost masculine delight in the sight of him. Her intense study of his body was incredibly erotic, and Tom didn't want to break the mood.

Lila dropped gently to her knees in front of him. Still keeping her eyes fixed on his body, she languidly tugged his briefs down, over his thighs, and finally to the floor. Tom clenched his jaw. He wanted to see her face, but Lila didn't look up.

"Hmmm." There it was again, that wordless sound of approval. Or maybe "Mmmm." He still couldn't be certain. Either way, the noise kicked his arousal up several more notches.

Without warning, Lila closed her mouth around him. The wet heat of her mouth made him groan. His knees nearly buckled, but Lila's hands, now on his buttocks, kept him standing. Blindly, Tom sought the edge of the counter with his hands to keep himself steady.

She made love to him with her mouth, a slow and steady movement that brought him to the edge within minutes. As if sensing his impending climax, she eased off and teased him with her lips and teeth. She cupped his rear and held him close, then moved him away from her.

Sweat broke out on his brow. His fingers were white-knuckled, gripping the edge of the counter. His other hand twined in her hair, tangling in her curls. It took great effort not to pull it hard enough to hurt her.

She was doing things to him that no woman had ever done, and it was better, more intense because it was Lila kneeling before him. The woman he loved. He moaned her name, and she paused to press a kiss just below the navel.

Tom could wait no longer. It was no longer good enough to receive such pleasure; he wanted to share it with Lila. No longer so careful not to pull too hard, he tugged her upward. She gasped, but the sound had more pleasure than pain in it.

With one swift movement, he lifted her onto the counter. Their mouths molded together, and her hands clutched his shoulders. Without breaking the kiss, Tom slid her long underwear down past her hips. He pushed them off her feet and into a tangled heap.

He slid into her with one smooth thrust that had them both groaning. Lila wrapped her legs around his hips, her arms stretched back behind her to support herself on the countertop. Her head was thrown back, and the sleek line of her throat begged for him to kiss her there.

They moved together like clockwork dancers freshly coated in oil. Every thrust into her slick heat had him wanting to last forever, but as Lila rocked her hips against him Tom knew he wasn't going to last even two minutes. He slipped his thumb against her swollen clitoris and pressed gently in counterpoint to his thrusts.

"Tom." Her eyes opened.

Tom brought his mouth down on hers again, though kissing her made the position awkward. Neither of them cared. They had reached the point where any movement could only increase their pleasure. The rocked together, Lila's fingers clawing now into his back.

She let out a cry that was different, and he knew she had reached her orgasm. The thought sent him spiraling into his own climax, and he whispered her name with his final thrust.

Her eyes met his. She was smiling. A thought sprang into his mind, and he saw the look in her eyes change at the same moment. She had thought the same thing.

"I didn't use anything."

Lila nodded. "I know."

They moved away from each other slightly so Lila could slide off the counter. She busied herself for a moment with the dishcloth he handed her. When she had finished and slid her pants back up around her waist, she turned to look at him.

"I'm on the pill."

Relief flooded him, but it was still no excuse. Not in today's world where loving someone could mean killing them. Tom folded her hand in his.

"A couple of years ago, I decided I wasn't going to sleep around anymore. I went to a walk-in clinic and had all the tests done. I'm clean. You're the first woman I've slept with in two years."

He saw relief in her eyes. "I haven't had any tests, Tom. But I haven't had unprotected sex—ever. Not once. No one's ever gotten me so carried away before." She grinned ruefully. "Until you."

They kissed again, and Tom marveled how easy it was to be with her.

"Hey." Lila finally broke away. "Didn't you promise me food?"

He had. It was short work to throw a couple of steaks on the grill, make a quick salad and open a bottle of wine. They ate like wolverines and finished the meal with two slices of cheesecake.

Lila patted her mouth with a napkin. "I'm stuffed."

They shared a grin. Conversation had flowed from one topic to the next without pause. It was nice to be so comfortable in each other's presence that neither was embarrassed.

"Lila, does it bother you that I'm not Jewish?" The question had been bothering him for some time.

For a long moment, she merely stared at him. "No one's ever asked me that before. Usually it's the other way around."

"Does it?"

She shook her head. "No. I don't think it matters what faith you are as long as you try to follow it the best you can. I'm not the greatest Jew in the world, Tom. I don't observe all the rules. But my faith is important to me. It isn't just not eating pork, or going to synagogue, or never sitting on Santa's lap. And it's not just having a bubbe instead of a grandma, or saying 'Oy!', or understanding Woody Allen movies either. It's not something I'll ever give up, if that's what you mean."

Awkwardness overtook him for a moment. "I don't go to church."

She smiled. "'That's okay by me."

"My family does, but I don't." He tried hard to say what he meant without sounding stupid, or worse, patronizing.

Now she was looking at him curiously. "It's okay, Tom. Really."

"I never dated anybody Jewish before." He nearly choked on the weight of his foot in his mouth.

Now she was frowning. "Maybe I should ask you if it bothers you."

"No!" He was making a mess of things. The last thing he wanted to do was spoil the mood. "No, Lila, that's not what I meant at all."

"Then what did you mean?"

"I just wanted to know if you cared that I wasn't because it could make a difference, couldn't it?" He paused. "I mean...if you wanted to marry someone who wasn't."

She licked a bite of cheesecake from the tines of her fork and studied him carefully. "I've always imagined I'd have a Jewish wedding. The wedding canopy, the bride circling the groom, the whole bit. And I never imagined having a Christmas tree in my house. I guess it is more important to me than I realized."

Tom wanted more than anything to be the smooth sophisticate so many people assumed he was. As it was, he was lucky his voice came out sounding normal instead of all crunched together and wobbly, the way he felt even bringing up the subject. Lila was looking at him curiously.

"I've never been to a Jewish wedding. Maybe I'll have to learn more about them."

She smiled slowly, her face turning rosy. "Maybe you will."

He linked the fingers of one of his hands through hers across the table. "What are we talking about, Lila?"

She squeezed his hand. "Hmm. I'm not sure. You tell me."

She had to know what he was hinting about. She was on his wavelength, just like she was with everything else. Suddenly, Tom grew giddy from staring into her eyes, from the subject of their conversation, from the food and the heat in the room...simply from being with Lila. He had to kiss her again just because she looked so lovely with steak sauce at the corner of her mouth.

But when he opened his mouth to tell her he loved her enough to ask her to be his wife, something inside him froze. He loved her; there was no fear about that. But asking her to marry him was something altogether different. Was he ready for that? Was she? Did he want to risk getting shot down now, when for the first time ever he had fallen so completely, head over heels for someone?

"Maybe I'll have to add matzo ball soup to the menu," he said instead of spilling his heart.

The instant the words left his mouth, he regretted them. He could tell by the look on Lila's face she had expected him to say something else. But she smiled when he did, allowing the moment to pass without comment.

He could see her eyes following the lines of his face. She touched his cheek softly, then his lips. She smiled again, though somewhat sadly.

"You are so beautiful," she murmured. "Everything about you is wonderful."

"You're beautiful, too."

She shook her head. "No. Not like you."

Tom clenched his fingers around hers. He forced her eyes to meet his. "You are beautiful to me. Don't ever let me hear you saying otherwise. You are pretty and smart and funny. You smell like heaven. You are the most wonderful woman I've ever known. Believe that."

She smiled, and this time it was genuine. Tears sparkled in her blue-ice eyes. She pressed his hand against her cheek. "I do."

He was sorry again he had wimped out, but there was nothing he could do. He leaned across the table to kiss the woman he loved. The moment had passed and his opportunity with it. He would have others. If only he could find the courage to make them.

CHAPTER 8

Lila snuggled further into the depths of her comforter. It was a glorious Saturday morning. She had hopped out only long enough to raise the shade before burrowing back beneath the heavy bedspread. Now, the bright sun shining through the window told her she had slept luxuriously late. Her flannel pajamas were soft and comfortable, her stomach wasn't rumbling, and she didn't have to go to the bathroom. She had no place to be and nothing to do. It was heaven.

Unfortunately, she had forgotten to turn off the ringer on the bedroom phone. Just as Lila was contemplating whether to go back to sleep or dive into the latest Stephen King novel she'd been saving as a special treat, the beastly thing rang. She could ignore it and allow the machine to pick up. After the fifth ring, she realized the brief power outages created by the blizzard had knocked the answering machine out of commission.

"Hello?" The tone was one she used for telephone solicitors.

"Lila-love!"

Rivka sounded slightly less hysterical than she had three days before, but only slightly so. Lila sighed. There went her peaceful Saturday morning. "What's wrong?"

"The opening!" Rivka moaned theatrically. "I'm sick about it."

Lila switched into soothing mode. "Riv, I thought you were okay. It's not for three weeks."

"This damn snow has the mail backed up! People aren't going to get their invitations in time to RSVP! My paintings are still in Pittsburgh and won't be shipped until next week! Then I have to hang them. The printer's been closed for three days, so my prints are behind schedule!"

Lila snuggled down into the covers. "Calm down. We have plenty of time. I heard a snow plow go by this morning, which means the streets are cleared. Things are going to be all right!"

"I need to talk to Tom."

Lila paused before replying. "You're assuming he's here."

"Isn't he?"

"No, Rivka. Tom is probably at The Foxfire. His business, remember? You're not the only one whose plans were messed up by the snow."

"Correct as usual, my dear, stable sister Lila." Rivka laughed. "Was I hysterical?"

"Slightly. Have Mickey slap you."

"Mickey?" Rivka snorted. "Lila, I tossed him out the door first thing this morning. Three days locked up together was just too much!"

Lila stretched against the flannel sheets. "Your opening is going to be wonderful. I thought I was supposed to be the worrier, Rivka."

Her sister snorted again. "I must have caught it from you."

There was no hope now of going back to sleep. Lila's stomach had begun rumbling, so there was no chance of curling up in bed with her new book either. She yawned, stretched, and swung her feet over the edge of the bed.

"Gotta go." She prepared to disconnect.

"Wait!"

Here came the interrogation. "Yes, we're dating. Yes, he spent the night. Yes, I'm going to see him today. That cover all the bases?"

"You know me too well." Rivka switched tactics. "Tom Caine is one of the nicest guys I know. I can't think why I didn't set you two up before."

"You didn't set us up!" Lila took the cordless phone with her, padded into the bathroom, and turned on the shower. "We met all on our own, thank you very much."

"Whatever. I'm just glad you're finally seeing someone worthwhile."

Lila refrained from replying to her sister's comment on her love life. "He's very nice, Rivka."

"Nice! Is that all you can say about him, is nice? The man's a god!"

Lila clucked her tongue in admonition. "I'm ashamed of you. Placing so much emphasis on a man's looks. There's a lot more to him than his face."

"I bet." Rivka chuckled. "Like about a good eight inches—"

Lila hung up the phone and cut off the rest of her sister's nosy imaginings. The shower was hot, steam pouring out. But Rivka's naughty words had got her to thinking. She'd probably be better off taking a cold shower instead.

She might have done just that, but for the fact that the

house was cold enough already. She had turned the heat up, but the power outages had wreaked havoc on more than just her answering machine; the temperamental furnace in her basement was working in spurts. If she really needed to cool down, all she had to do was stand around in her nightgown for a few minutes.

As the bathroom filled with welcome warmth, Lila's shiver had little to do with the cranky furnace. The chill running down her spine had everything to do with Tom. She stepped into the shower, and the nearly too-hot water cascaded over her body. It was touching her in all the places Tom had recently touched, and Lila couldn't hold back the tiny groan as she remembered.

The blizzard that had shut down central Pennsylvania for the past three days had been a perfect mini-vacation. As Darren had predicted, nobody could get into work. The state police, in fact, had issued an order that only emergency personnel would be allowed on the streets at all for forty-eight hours.

For Tom and Lila, it was the perfect excuse to spend every spare minute together. Though he had stopped back at his place for some fresh clothes and to tell his niece where he'd be, Tom had been staying at Lila's since the day they'd made love in the restaurant. They had stayed up late watching old movies on television and eating popcorn popped in Lila's fireplace. They had engaged in a fierce Monopoly tournament that left Tom bankrupt and Lila the proud owner of both Boardwalk and Park Place. They had talked for hours and shared stories from every part of their lives. And they had made love.

Lila had never felt so close to a man. It was more than the way Tom knew how to touch her body; it was the way he had learned to touch her heart. He only had to look at her it seemed, to know what she was thinking. He had begun to finish her sentences.

It didn't matter any more what he looked like. He wasn't a pair of broad shoulders or startling hazel eyes anymore. He was just Tom.

That didn't mean the sight of him bare-chested still didn't make her catch her breath. She worked the lather through her thick curls. He could still weaken her knees with just a look.

What had started out as lust had quickly become so much more. She had meant it to be a not-quite casual affair, a chance to satisfy her body's insistent urges. She'd never meant to risk her heart.

Too late now, she thought. She was in deep, maybe way over her head, but there was nothing to be done. She loved him, head over heels. What she felt for Tom was light years beyond what she'd had with William.

No supermodel would ever stare at her from out of the mirror, and she would probably never fit into her high-school prom dress again, but none of that mattered. Tom had shown her what he thought was precious and lovely had nothing to do with what shade of lipstick she wore or whether she looked good in stiletto pumps. She only had to be herself. If it was enough for him, then it was damn sure good enough for her.

He had left early this morning, determined to get The Foxfire back into operating condition by this afternoon. After so many days cooped up at home, most people would be dying to get out and do something, and Tom wanted to be prepared. He had called all the staff last night to let them know what time to be in and left in plenty of time to head back to his house and change before going to the restaurant.

Lila rinsed off and stepped out of the shower. Though

the past three days had been wonderful, she, too, was looking forward to getting out. Tom had promised her lunch today, but she probably wouldn't see much of him. He devoted a lot of himself to his business, and she respected that. Still, the promise of seeing him even briefly had her heart skipping a beat. She wanted to sing. And, as she toweled off and began dressing to meet the man who had changed her mind about pretty faces, that's exactly what she did.

Silence met Tom when he entered his house. He'd left Lila sleeping, waking her just long enough to promise her lunch at The Foxfire today. The roads had mostly been cleared, so he was able to jog back to his house in record time. He wanted to shower, change, and grab some breakfast before heading over to the restaurant. It was going to be a crazy day.

Not wanting to wake Emma, he climbed the stairs two at a time as quietly as he could. He'd phoned her last night along with the rest of the staff to let them all know he expected them to show up for work on Saturday morning. Still, it was pretty early. Emma really didn't have to be in for another couple of hours.

Darkness shrouded the hallway, but Tom didn't bother turning on a light. He knew exactly where he was going, and...WHAM!

Tom hit someone coming out of Emma's room. It wasn't Emma, not unless she'd shot up about five inches and put on forty pounds. The intruder grunted and went down after the impact.

Heart hammering, Tom tried to remember the self-defense techniques he'd learned at the YMCA a few years back. Letting out a thundering yell, he thrust his fists out in front of him and stamped down on the interloper with all his weight. The man on the ground let out a loud yelp of pain.

"If you've hurt Emma, I'll kill you!" Tom roared, keeping his stance. Though he wanted to see who was lurking in his upstairs hallway, the shadows still obscured the man's face. He didn't want to get too close to the downed invader in case the man was planning to spring up and hit him. "I may just kill you anyway!"

The hall suddenly lit up like a county fair. Tom blinked in the brightness, opening one fist to shield his eyes from the glare. Emma's door, directly to his right, had opened, and his niece came flying out.

"Mike!" she shrieked, bending over the prone man on the floor. "Boss! You moron, you've killed him!"

To protect the area Tom had stomped, Michel Leroy curled into a tight ball in the hallway. His face was pasty white with a greenish tinge. Emma bent over him and fluttered her hands over his face. When she saw just where Michel had been injured, she glared up at her uncle with undisguised dismay.

"Boss, you stomped him in the nuts," she scolded. "What kind of fair fighting is that?"

Tom was confused. His heartbeat slowed and he lowered his fists. "Emma, he came out at me in the dark. What was I supposed to do?"

"...take a shower." Michel wheezed as Emma helped him sit up. His color was returning to normal, but he still cradled his injured parts tenderly.

"He was going to the bathroom."

"He ran into me." Tom was still in shock about the whole incident. "How was I supposed to know who it was?"

Emma grunted. "You still didn't have to kick him where it counts. That's low, boss, really low."

Michel struggled to his feet. His face had gone from greenish white to slowly darkening brick red. Tom realized the man was blushing.

"I apologize." He sounded like a man who'd just had his fingers...or something...slammed in a door. "For coming into your house and defiling your niece."

"What?" Tom and Emma both said at the same time.

Emma turned on Michel and slapped his arm. "Don't tell him that!"

"Yeah, don't tell me that."

Tom winced. The whole situation was getting more and more ridiculous. The last thing he wanted to hear about was his twenty-four-year-old niece's love life. There were just some things in life that were off-limits.

"But Emma, I must tell your oncle the truth—"

"Don't listen to him, boss." Emma clapped her hand across Michel's mouth. "He didn't do any defiling."

"I really don't want to know." All Tom wanted to do was head for his own room, take a shower, and get down to The Foxfire. He didn't want to stand in his hallway with his chef and sous-chef, both of whom, he now saw with increasing discomfort, were in an embarrassing state of undress.

"Mike, don't go all chauvinistic on me. I invited you here, I made you stay the night, and I'm the one who seduced you."

"All right!" The conversation had gone way beyond what Tom wanted to hear. "I don't care why Michel is here,

Emma. I just want to take a shower and get to the restaurant. Okay?"

"Sheesh." Emma wrapped her arm around Michel's waist. "What's gotten into you?"

Tom shook his head and threw his hands in the air. "Emma, don't make me explain."

As he headed down the hallway toward his bedroom, he heard Emma's giggle. It was followed by the unmistakable sound of two people kissing and the click of Emma's door shutting. As Tom ducked in his own doorway, he couldn't stop a grin. His niece had finally cornered Michel Leroy.

Lila pushed through the front doors of The Foxfire, which was even more crowded than usual. Then again, half the city had probably turned out today to fill their bellies with food they hadn't had to open from cans. The smell of blackened fish wafted to her as a waitress passed by with a platter, and Lila's stomach rumbled. She was looking forward to something good to eat.

The walk hadn't hurt her appetite either. Still, as she searched for Tom in the crowd, her stomach jumped with more than hunger. Her gaze roamed the restaurant, and she searched for his familiar profile. She was hungry for something, and it wasn't just food.

"One for lunch?"

It was the same hostess as before, the blonde with the expertly made-up face. She stared rather blankly at Lila. Her exquisitely plucked brows furrowed ever so slightly as if she thought she should recognize Lila, but didn't. Nothing, however, could daunt Lila today, not even Ms. Plastic-Perfect.

"I'm here to see Tom Caine."

The blonde's eyes cleared. Not by very much, Lila noted somewhat meanly, but enough to show some light was clicking on underneath the blonde hair. The hostess smiled with false sincerity.

"Is he expecting you?" Her tone clearly indicated she didn't think that was a possibility.

Lila lifted her chin slightly and vowed not to let the woman get under skin. "Yes, he is actually."

The blonde hostess's smile broadened, as if she found Lila's reply amusing. "Are you sure? He's very busy today."

Lila's mouth began to thin into a scowl, but she forced herself to keep her tone light. "Of course I'm sure." She paused to read the other woman's nametag. "Jennifer. He invited me here himself. He told me to meet him at noon. Please just tell him I'm here."

Jennifer's expertly shaped brows rose slightly and her bright smile faltered. "Of course." Her tone sounded wounded as if Lila had been unquestionably rude to her. "Let me go see if I can find him."

She disappeared into the back so briefly Lila knew she couldn't have looked very long.

"He seems to be unavailable just now." Jennifer smirked. "Please sit down while you wait."

Lila did so, if only because she didn't want to make a scene. Several people had come into the restaurant behind her, and she didn't want them to leave while she argued with Jennifer. The Foxfire was Tom's business after all, and she didn't want to lose him any customers.

Several minutes passed while Jennifer graciously took the names of diners and directed those whose tables were ready to their seats. The blonde had nothing but smiles for every man who came in, and Lila's hostility grew. To women, especially those who were alone, the hostess was cooler, though not in any way you could really put your finger on. It was more the things she didn't say, the smiles she didn't give, than it was anything she actually said or did.

The hostess seemed to have forgotten about Lila, who was just deciding to push her way back to Tom's office when one of the waitresses came around the corner. Pausing at the podium behind which Jennifer reigned, the waitress glanced at Lila. Lila pretended not to notice and instead contemplated the threads of her coat.

"Wendi." Jennifer's blue gaze flicked Lila's way. "Pretty busy today?"

Wendi flipped her waist-length, chestnut braid over her shoulder. The uniform of white shirt and black skirt, which managed to make the rest of the staff look crisp and professional, fit her like she was an exotic dancer. She had the body to be one. The waiting area had suddenly grown very warm.

"Rilly." Wendi's voice was a cliché.

Both women looked covertly at Lila. Jennifer seemed barely able to refrain from bursting out laughing, and Wendi was unable to keep a smirk from turning up her glossy lips. Lila had the uncomfortable feeling they were mocking her.

"Have you been able to find Tom?" Jennifer asked loudly, making certain Lila could hear. "Someone's waiting for him."

"No, Jen, he's not in the kitchen. He's in his office, talking to Donna. They've been in there a really long time." Wendi lowered her voice theatrically, but still spoke clearly enough that Lila could hear her every word. "You know how long it always takes for him to talk to Donna."

Lila's fingers curled against her palms. Her stomach,

which had been impatiently growling a few minutes before, now began an uneasy flip-flopping. She forced a look of blank composure on her face; she didn't want Jennifer and Wendi to think she was listening to them.

"I guess that's why she's head waitress." Wendi made a great show of studying her long, polished nails. "She sure gets a lot of on-the-job training."

Wendi and Jennifer shared a smirk then and both glanced sideways at Lila. She continued studying the menu, her coat, her fingernails, and anything that would give them the impression she was patiently waiting and nothing more. "Maybe someone should go knock on his door." Jennifer's last word sounded suspiciously like a giggle.

Wendi rolled her eyes. "Not me, thanks."

Again, Lila struggled not to let her face show she was listening. Lila told herself she had no reason to be suspicious. After all, she trusted him. Didn't she?

"Someone's waiting for him." This time Jennifer said it loudly enough Lila couldn't mistake the words were meant for her ears. The blonde hostess' voice dropped, but not far enough. "Looks like a real charity case."

Lila's stomach lurched to her throat. The room became suddenly, stiflingly hot. Charity case! The words hammered her eardrums hard enough to block out the rest of what the two women were saying. Charity case! The comment rang over and over, causing her head to spin.

Lila staggered to her feet. She blinked rapidly, trying to clear her gaze from the red ooze that seemed to be swimming in her vision. She needed air, and she needed it fast. She needed to get away from The Foxfire.

"Can I help you?" Jennifer's giggles seemed under control for the moment. She tapped her long nails against one of the plastic-coated menus.

"I'm afraid I can't wait for Tom any longer." Lila's voice trembled, and she clenched her nails into her palms. The sting gave her some strength. "Please tell him Lila couldn't wait for him any more."

"Sure," Jennifer cooed. "You don't look good, sweetie. You look like you need some air."

Lila bit her tongue to stifle a nasty retort. She hated being called "sweetie" by someone she didn't even know. That Jennifer was obviously laughing at her distress only made matters worse.

"Just a little too warm," Lila bit out tersely.

As she pushed her way out the front doors, she thought she heard a cackle of nasty laughter behind her. The cold air hit her like a slap and rocked her head back. It felt wonderful.

She fought the hot tears slipping over her cheeks. If there had been a breeze, they might have dried quickly, but the air was frigid and still. The tears froze to her face as solidly as they froze in her heart.

It was five o'clock before Tom had a moment to sit down and breathe. The blizzard had messed up deliveries all over central Pennsylvania, and he'd had to make a lot of last-minute changes in the Saturday specials. Plus, the crowds had been overwhelming. The Foxfire had run out of onion soup, garlic bread, and salmon steaks by one-thirty p.m., and various other things over the rest of the afternoon. Fortunately, most people were just so glad to be out of their houses they willingly accepted substitutions.

He propped his feet up on his desk with a sigh that

came from his toes. Stretching out the kinks in his back, Tom looked at the clock. Blinking, he took another look.

He had promised Lila lunch today. True, he'd been so busy he hadn't even had time to notice the lunch hour come and go, but surely she would have asked someone to find him. Frowning, he dialed Lila's phone number.

The answering machine beeped, but no message played in his ear. He knew the power outages had done some damage to it, and he guessed she hadn't had time to fix it yet. He would take the chance that the machine would record his voice.

"Lila, it's me." He didn't bother to identify himself further because he knew he didn't have to. It was a good feeling. No, a great feeling. "Sorry I missed you today. What happened? Call me when you get in. I'm heading home."

The fact she hadn't shown up or called still disturbed him, but he shrugged off the feeling. Maybe something had come up with her sister. Maybe she'd stopped by, seen how busy he was and didn't want to bother him. Whatever had happened, he was sure he'd see her tonight. They'd talked about renting a really good scary movie, popping some corn, and hanging out at his place for a change. Lila had never been to his house, and he wanted her to meet Emma.

"Boss, can I talk to you?" Emma stood in the doorway. Chocolate sauce, flour, and a dozen other substances Tom couldn't identify dotted her white smock.

"Sure, Em. What's up?"

She closed the door behind her and plopped down in the soft chair across from him. "It's about this morning."

Tom held up his hands. "Say no more. You're both adults."

Emma sighed. "Tell my mom that, will ya?"

Tom grinned. His older sister Marietta was not known

for her open mind or lenient attitude. "I'm not telling your mom anything, Emma. When you came to live with me, she made me promise I'd look out for you. I'm not going to risk my hide by telling her I found a half-naked man coming out of your bedroom."

"Uncle Tom, you're so cool." Emma leaned over the table to kiss his cheek with a loud smack. "I wish Mom were more like you."

"Uncles can be cool. Parents have to play the heavy." The philosophical tone made his niece roll her eyes.

"That coming from the man who swore he'd never 'sow his seed,' to quote you from about a year ago."

Tom remembered saying that. It had been to Marietta, in fact, at the annual Caine family get-together. She'd cornered him and wanted to know why he'd come dateless, when was he going to settle down, and why didn't he think about giving Mom some more grandkids? He'd replied with the comment Emma had just quoted. Marietta hadn't seen the humor in his reply.

"Things change." Her eyes sparkling and her grin wrinkling her freckled nose, Emma pounced toward him. "Boss, you're in love!"

Tom shrugged but couldn't hide his own grin. "Maybe."

Emma shrieked. "With the one you spent the blizzard with?"

He raised his eyebrow at her. "Her name is Lila, and yes. And don't go telling your mother about where I spent the blizzard."

Emma quickly drew an X on her chest with one finger. "She won't hear it from my lips. God forbid I stay home alone at the ripe old age of twenty-four. So, tell me about her!"

What could he say about Lila? There was too much, all

mixed up inside with the feelings he'd never thought to experience. He couldn't describe her because words could simply not do her justice.

"She's great." That would not be enough for Emma. "I can talk to her."

"Wow." Emma sounded as solemn as if he'd recited a sonnet in Lila's honor. "I've never heard you say that about anyone before. She must be great. And crazy."

"Why crazy?"

"To fall for you." Emma danced out of his grasp.

"No crazier than Michel." Tom cowered under Emma's flurry of tiny punches. "Hey, stop that, Squirt!"

His use of the dreaded nickname from the past stopped Emma in her tracks. "Don't call me that!"

Tom, who knew just how to tease his niece into a frenzy, replied calmly, "Squirt."

Emma shrieked again, launching herself over the desk at him to pummel him soundly. Tom responded by twisting her arm up behind her back and tickling her mercilessly. Both ended by laughing hysterically.

"So when can I meet Lila the Great?"

"How about tonight? She's supposed to come over and watch a movie."

Emma nodded. "Cool. Maybe I'll ask Mike to come over, too. It can be a double date."

A discreet knock came at the door. Jennifer stuck her head inside, her brilliant smile fading a bit when she saw Emma. The spunky redhead took that as her cue to leave and pressed another kiss to Tom's cheek.

"Tom." Jennifer's voice was smooth. "Wendi and I are going to Wanda's Beach Club after work. Do you want to come?"

"Thanks, Jen, but I've got other plans." Wanda's was a

meat market that Tom had never liked. The thought of going there with Jennifer and Wendi made him shudder.

Already the thought of curling up on his battered sofa with Lila was making him smile. They'd make some popcorn. Maybe they'd play a board game with Emma and Michel. It was the kind of domesticated evening that would have made him run screaming into the night only several months ago, but with Lila, it seemed perfect.

Jennifer pouted. "Too bad. We've missed you coming out with us, Tom."

He shrugged. Jennifer's wide-eyed gaze and pouty smile were starting to wear thin. She was acting as though the few times he'd seen her socially had been dates, which they most adamantly weren't. Tom didn't do anything beyond casual flirtation with anybody he worked with.

"Got other plans."

She just didn't seem to be getting the hint.

"A hot date?" Her voice made it clear that any date not with her couldn't possibly be hot enough.

"Just renting a movie."

"Alone?"

For some reason, he didn't want to tell Jennifer he was planning on staying in with Lila. It was just the sort of private information that could lead to rumors around the restaurant, and he didn't want that. Besides, what he did on his own time was his own affair. More than that, he had an idea telling Jennifer about Lila would only lead to more questions he didn't feel like answering.

"Yeah."

"Okay for you." Jennifer shrugged. "You're going to miss out on a great night. Tonight's the wet T-shirt contest."

Tom managed a smile. "I'll survive."

"If you say so." She left the office. Tom hooked his coat

from the rack and grabbed his keys. The evening manager, Frank Philips, had already come on duty, so The Foxfire was under control. As he slipped out the back exit and into the parking lot, however, Tom discovered he wasn't going to be heading straight home after all. The Foxfire back lot edged up against the parking lot to the building housing offices for one of Harrisburg's most prestigious law firms. Typically, the building was dark and the lot empty at this time, but tonight Tom saw a dark-colored Lexus still there. It was parked facing him, just a few spaces away from the Tahoe.

The car's presence was a little strange. He headed toward his truck, but it wasn't until he saw a brief flash of white from the Lexus' passenger side that he could tell how strange. As Tom got closer, he realized with some surprise the flash he'd seen was flesh. Bare flesh.

The Lexus was moving a little, rocking slightly back and forth in a very characteristic way. Now that he drew nearer the car, Tom could see its windows were steamed up. Another flash of white, and this time he recognized it as a foot pressing against the front windshield.

Now he was uncomfortable. In order to get to his truck, he'd have to pass right by the Lexus, close enough to see inside. Whoever was in there wouldn't appreciate an audience, of that Tom was certain. He was debating whether to slink by with eyes averted or go back to The Foxfire and catch a cab when the Lexus' front door opened and a woman almost tumbled out.

She was, Tom was immensely relieved to note, clothed. Not fully, and certainly not well enough for the cold weather, but she wasn't naked. A tall, chesty brunette, the woman leaned against the car and began taking long, deep drags on her cigarette. She didn't notice Tom.

"Get back in here!" a male voice demanded from inside the car. "You want someone to see you?"

The brunette stuck up her middle finger at him. "If you won't let me smoke in the car then I gotta do it outside. And I ain't giving up my after-sex cigarette just 'cause your wife's got a nose like a bloodhound."

"Tammy, please get back inside." The man in the car poked his head out the door.

He was a handsome man with classic features and a full head of sandy hair. He looked like a polo player. He was probably one of the lawyers from next door.

"Billy!" Tammy's voice became an annoying whine. "Just let me have my smoke."

Billy saw Tom at that moment. The man's handsome face turned as pinched as a dried apple, and he barked at Tammy to get back in the car before he drove off without her. Turning to see what exactly had her paramour in such a state, Tammy spied Tom watching.

"Pervert." She sniffed and slid back into the Lexus, which roared into life immediately.

As the car sped from the parking lot, Tom caught another glimpse of the car's passengers. He looked like he'd been eating sour fruit. Tammy, on the other hand, was smiling.

Shaking his head, Tom slipped behind the wheel of his Tahoe. Some people. He was glad he and Lila didn't have to resort to that sort of behavior. Lila. At the thought, he pressed his foot to the floor and headed for home.

CHAPTER 9

Tom hung up the phone and cracked his knuckles nervously. Where could she be? She had left no message, not on his machine at home or at the restaurant. He knew because he had called to be sure. She had obviously not been home recently because her machine was full. He hadn't even been able to leave a message this time.

He had called the gallery, but got no answer. Mick and Rivka's line, too, rang on and on before their machine had picked up. They were probably all together. Maybe Lila had forgotten their plans.

He was only trying to make himself feel better. The fact was Lila had either stood him up or something had happened to prevent her from returning his call. Both scenarios made his stomach churn.

Crunching another set of antacid tablets, Tom began pacing his living room. The television was on, blaring, but he barely noticed. He had gone ahead to the video store and picked up several good horror movies. Not one of them appealed to him now. Not when he was becoming more and more fearful something bad had happened to Lila.

The thought of Lila lying white and silent in a hospital bed made him sit down suddenly. He cracked his knuckles some more, a nervous habit that drove Emma crazy. She wasn't there to complain, however. She and Michel had decided to take the two-hour drive to visit her parents. Under other circumstances, Tom would have been quite happy for his niece, but tonight all he could think about was Lila. Where was she?

Sitting around his house wasn't going to do anything but give him an ulcer. His stomach already felt like it was on fire, even though he'd crunched up half a roll of antacids. He decided to go to her house. Even if she wasn't there, he could wait for her.

As soon as he'd made his decision, Tom began to feel better. Anything would be better than waiting for the phone to ring, even sitting in the cold on Lila's front porch. At least this way, he'd be there when she got home. A sudden, chilling thought struck him. Unless she already was home.

One of the videos he'd rented seemed to scream out at him. *Afraid of the Dark* was a cheesy, low-budget horror flick about a young woman who lived alone, attacked by a maniac hiding in her basement. Tom had rented the movie because of its melodramatic title and cover art. Now, thinking of Lila, he flung the video onto the floor.

Heart pounding, he pulled on an extra sweatshirt. Going to the hall closet, he found heavy woolen gloves with a matching hat and scarf. It was bound to be cold while waiting, but he knew he wouldn't mind. He'd wait until his fingers and toes fell off as long as it meant Lila was all right.

Maybe she'd been in an accident. Tom froze again, his stomach lurching ominously. He had always been cursed with an oversensitive stomach and an overactive imagination. Both were working overtime tonight. Forcing away the image of Lila's car crushed beneath the tires of an eighteen-wheeler, he continued dressing.

He would try phoning her one last time. Perhaps she had gotten home in the half hour since he'd last called. The phone rang and rang, but this time the machine did pick up. As he left another message, Tom's queasy stomach began settling slightly. She had been home to get her messages.

Unless the man hiding in her basement had checked the machine for her.

"Lila? Honey, it's me. Please call me right away. I'm worried sick about you."

Hanging up, he decided to head over there anyway. He couldn't sit here and wait for her to call him back. The tension was unbearable.

Just as he reached the front door, the bell rang. Lila! It must be! Eagerly, Tom flung open the heavy carved door without even bothering to look out the window.

"Hi, Tom," Jennifer said with a bright grin.

Wendi was with her. Both wore micro-miniskirts: Jen's in vibrant red, and Wendi's in harsh lime green, and both wore black leather jackets that looked none too warm. Both were shivering, and no wonder, Tom noted. Neither wore stockings of any kind. Their bare feet were shoved into the highest stiletto heels he'd ever seen.

"Can we come in?" Wendi's teeth chattered. "It's freezing out here."

Too surprised to see them to think about turning them away, Tom stepped aside to let them in. Surrounded by a cloud of perfume so strong it made his eyes water, the women pushed past him and into the living room. He closed the door firmly and followed them.

"I was just on my way out." He waved one glove to show he, at least, was dressed for the weather.

"Oh, just let us stay long enough to warm up," Jennifer pleaded. "We only wanted to come by and keep you company. You did say you were going to be alone tonight."

He had said that, but hadn't thought it was going to be true. He'd been looking forward to a nice, relaxing evening with Lila. Instead, he'd spent the night dialing the phone and worrying himself into a frenzy.

"Mind if we take off our coats?" Wendi slipped hers off without waiting for an answer. Beneath it she wore a shirt of some shimmery material that matched her skirt.

Tom blinked twice, slowly. Wendi wasn't wearing a bra beneath the shirt, which glimmered in the light just enough to camouflage the fact it was almost totally sheer. And she was cold; he could definitely see that.

"You have such a nice house." Jennifer, too, slung off her leather coat. Though the shirt she wore wasn't as transparent as Wendi's, it left nothing to the imagination either. Her nipples were hard points poking through the silky white fabric, and Tom realized he could see the dusky ring of her aureoles through the cloth. He swallowed heavily.

"Thanks." Suddenly, in his heavy layers of clothing, he felt much too warm.

Both women sat down—Jennifer at one end of the couch, and Wendi on the big, overstuffed chair beside her. Almost in unison, the tiny scraps of material they dared to call skirts rose up equally high on thighs tanned the golden color of wheat. Both crossed their legs at the same time, almost as though they had scripted every movement beforehand.

"Where were you going, Tom?" Wendi's voice was husky. She swung her leg up and down, up and down, displaying the sculpted muscles in her calves to perfection.

He loosened the scarf around this throat. "To see a friend."

He was being subjected to a double onslaught of predatory femininity, and he was feeling a little light-headed. He knew he should tell both of them to just get out, but he was having trouble forming the words. He felt like a snake fixed in a mongoose's glare.

"Ooh." Jennifer breathed, wriggling a little on the couch. Her movement hitched her skirt up even higher. "Anyone we know?"

"I don't think so." He blinked, and suddenly the spell the two hot-to-trot vixens were trying to cast was broken. Of course they didn't know Lila. Women like Jen and Wendi wouldn't know someone like Lila. Women like the ones on his couch didn't deserve to know someone like Lila.

"Why not just stay here with us?" Wendi suggested. "It's too cold out there, Tom. It's nice and warm in here. With us."

Her words made him wrinkle his mouth with distaste. They thought they were being seductive. They didn't realize they were only being ridiculous.

"It was nice of you to stop by." His voice clearly showed he was being insincere. "But you'll have to leave. I'm on my way out."

Wendi and Jennifer exchanged startled looks. Obviously, they had overestimated their charm. Regaining her seductive smile, Jennifer turned to Tom.

"Are you sure?" She ran her tongue suggestively along her plump, glossy lips.

"Jennifer, I've never been more sure of anything," Tom said grimly.

Now the looks the two women exchanged were more

than startled. They were shocked. Wendi's mouth opened and closed like a codfish, and Jennifer's pretty features turned a bright red. Tom wagered to himself it was the first time the woman had blushed in years.

Wendi began to sputter. Jennifer, however, recovered more quickly. She hauled herself out of the depths of the couch, not bothering to pull her skirt past her thighs. The sight left Tom cold.

Jennifer didn't appear to notice because she insinuated herself into his arms before he could pull away. "Don't be shy. We already decided we're more than willing to share you."

Her glossy lips slid along his cheek, missing his mouth, but not by much. She reached up to run her hands through his hair, pulling it down over his eyes. Shaking his head, Tom grabbed her forearms and pushed her away, gently but firmly. "I think you'd better leave."

"Every man's fantasy," Jen persisted, her voice a low, husky and sex-soaked purr.

She refused to move far enough away from him, so he stepped back and let go. Without his hands to support her, she teetered on her stiletto heels. Jen flung her hair over her shoulder with the air of a haughty princess.

"Don't pretend you don't want it," she snapped, using the tip of her finger to dab her smudged lips. "There are men who'd give both their balls to fuck me and Wendi."

"Then I'd suggest you go and find one of them," Tom replied. "Because I'm not interested."

That, finally, seemed to deflate her, but only for an instant. With another hair toss, Jen beckoned to her friend. "C'mon, Wendi. It's obvious we're not wanted."

She couldn't have been more right, but Tom had been raised better than to agree aloud. He stepped aside to let them reach the door and ignored Wendi's quivering lip and Jen's furious sniffs. Just as they were pulling up the zippers on their form-fitting jackets to their heavily made up chins, the doorbell rang. Tom groaned, glancing at the clock. It was eleven o'clock on Saturday night. Time enough for all the sharks in the world to have slammed down a few margaritas and get sentimental about "the one that got away." Who was it this time? He flung the door open violently, prepared to tell the would-be seductress who awaited to stop wasting her time and go home.

It was Lila.

"Tom, I—" Lila broke off as she saw he wasn't alone. Two sleek manes of hair, one blonde and one brunette, appeared in the hall behind him. Both were attached to pretty faces and knockout bodies dressed in little more than underwear.

"Excuse us. We were just leaving." Jennifer pushed her way past Tom. She stopped when she saw Lila, and a thin smirk curved her glistening lips. "Oh, look, Wendi. It's Tom's charity case. Sorry, honey, he's already given at the office."

Lila looked at Tom's stricken face, the smudge of lip gloss, his disheveled hair. That, coupled with the women's smug looks and lack of clothes told her more than she needed to know. Without another word, Lila turned and left Tom's front porch. She managed not to slip on the icy walk, got into her car, and put the key in the ignition.

Lila stared steadfastly behind her as she backed out of the driveway. She guessed he was calling after her, but she couldn't hear him. Jennifer's words were ringing too loudly in her ears for her to hear anything else. She concentrated grimly on navigating the still-snowy streets. She had spent the afternoon wallowing in self-pity brought on by the blonde's nasty comments at The Foxfire. The phrase "charity case" had brought back every awful memory about her time with William. It had taken an entire quart of Superchocolate ice ream and a long, hot bath before she'd been able to face the thought of confronting Tom.

She'd swallowed her fear and her pride and gone to his house to tell him she loved him. She'd been greeted by something out of her worst nightmare. Her mind told her to give him a chance to explain, but her heart had put petal to the metal and driven her away into the night.

She was only a few blocks from her house when she suddenly decided she didn't want to go back. Not to the empty house, where the temptation to give in to self-pity might overwhelm her. Instead of turning left at the traffic light, she turned right. The night was young, and so was she. She had soaked in a steaming tub, washed her hair, and put on makeup. She'd shaved her legs, for God's sake, and she wasn't going to waste her time at home watching bad movies on cable TV. She was going to go out and forget Tom Caine.

"This wasn't exactly what I had in mind when I decided to surround myself with good-looking men." Lila looked around the crowded club.

Darren laughed loud and hard. "Honey, this is exactly the place you need to be. Ain't nothing more soothing than being surrounded by a bunch of super hot guys."

Lila couldn't help tapping her toes to the disco beat filling the nightclub. "Yeah, that's such a problem for me normally."

"Stop right there." Darren snapped his fingers. "I didn't fix your makeup and take you out just so I could listen to you be all nasty to yourself. If that Mr. Gorgeous can't tell a good thing when he's got it, then he doesn't deserve it."

"Thanks, Darren. That's what I needed to hear."

She leaned across her stool to plant a kiss on his caramel-colored cheek. Darren returned the buss, smacking his lips loudly on one side of her face, then the other. Lila began to feel better.

"Moving in on my main squeeze?" thundered a male voice from behind them.

"Sorry." Lila moved aside to let Lance slide onto the bar stool beside her.

"Not you," Lance kidded, squeezing her gently. "I meant him. Darren, don't make me get up in your face. You may have known her longer, but she's my boss lady tonight."

"He thinks he's the black Mr. Clean." Darren rolled his eyes.

Looking at Lance's shaved head, tiny gold earring, and white T-shirt with rolled sleeves, Lila could definitely see the resemblance. The thought made her giggle until Lance looked at her from wounded eyes. Then she kissed his cheek, too.

"Don't fight over me, boys," she said archly. "There's enough of me to go around."

Darren hooted and Lance chuckled. Lila slid off the bar stool and grabbed each of them by the arm. She was surprised to find herself feeling better.

"C'mon. You promised you'd take me dancing."

"Have I ever broken a promise to you?"

She shook her head, held out her hands, and let them pull her onto the floor. "Not yet."

"And I don't aim to tonight, honey! Let's dance!"

Lila had never moved so fast for so long. The music went on and on without stopping; one beat merging with the next so she couldn't even tell where one song ended and the next began. The dance floor was crowded, bodies crushing against each other, but everyone moved to the same rhythm. Sweat poured down her face and streaked the careful makeup Darren had applied earlier, but Lila didn't care. All that mattered was the sound of the drums and guitars gave her no time to think. No chance to let her mind fill with images of Tom.

Closing time came too quickly for Lila. As the club lights came on and people slowly began filtering out onto the street, Lila was filled with an exhaustion that, while not quite happy, at least was better than the draining lassitude she'd experienced earlier in the day.

The music didn't slow, but she did. At last Lila had to beg defeat, protesting when Darren and Lance both insisted on buying her yet another drink and taking her for one more twirl around the dance floor.

"I can't. Really. I'm exhausted!"

"You going to be all right?" Darren held the door open for Lila as they left the club with Lance.

"Fine." She yawned. "I'm going home and going straight to bed."

"We can go with you, if you want." Lance suddenly looked less like Mr. Clean and more like a very angry Marine. "In case that jerk is waiting for you."

Lila hadn't even thought of that. "No, that's okay. I'll be fine."

Darren pulled her close for a hug. "You call me if you need anything."

She nodded. "I will, but I won't."

Darren shook his head. "Honey, what's scary is I understood that."

"Go home," Lila urged her friends. "I'll be fine."

She got in her car while they watched and drove away with them still looking after her. It was nice to have friends. She was glad she had stopped by Darren's apartment, and even gladder she'd caught him before he went out for the night.

Rivka would be furious Lila hadn't called her first, of course, but she just hadn't wanted to face her sister. Tomorrow would be soon enough to let Rivka know the romance with Tom had gone the way of the dodo. Extinct. She'd been a fool to think telling him she loved him would make everything work out all right.

Love. How long could it last in the face of the constant attention he received? The never-ending snide looks and catty comments? How long would it be before she started to get suspicious, resentful...jealous? How long could their relationship last under pressure like that? Not very long. Lila bit back a sigh and forced her eyes to blink away the tears threatening. She was absolutely exhausted.

When she climbed the stairs to her front porch, however, what she saw made her snap instantly awake. She'd tossed a plastic cover over her porch swing to protect it from the elements. The cover now hung over the railing. Below the swing, in the snow she had not yet had the energy or desire to sweep away, were two man-sized footprints.

What really had her heart hammering, though, was not the boot prints in the snow, but the words traced next to them:

LILA, I LOVE YOU. CALL ME.

Lila reached for the mangled broom she kept in one

corner of the porch. The words were gone in seconds, along with the boot marks. Lila went inside.

The answering machine was blinking in double-time, an indication the tape was full. She'd had a lot of calls. Her finger hesitated over the button that would play the messages, but she didn't push it. Maybe Tom had an excuse for what she'd seen tonight, and maybe he didn't. At any rate, Lila wasn't ready to hear it. When the morning came and bright light with it, maybe this whole damn situation wouldn't seem so dark...but then again, it might. After walking over to the outlet on the wall, Lila unplugged the machine with a hard jerk of her wrist.

"Oops," she said without humor. "Power outage."

Then she went upstairs and got into bed.

Tom had waited on Lila's front porch for hours, until he could no longer feel his feet or his hands. He had watched all the lights in the neighboring houses go out, one by one, and still she hadn't come home. Damn it, where could she be?

Now, lying in his lonely bed, he continued shivering from being outside for so long. Though he'd taken a steaming shower, he still felt as though someone had dumped a truckload of ice cubes around him. Not even the memory of the look on Jennifer's and Wendi's faces when he told them to get lost could warm him...because the cold was on the inside. He was cold from eyebrows to toenails because of the look on Lila's face when he'd opened his door.

He cursed aloud for having let the women inside. He knew how it must have looked. He had heard the whole story behind the "charity case" comment, too, and even though he understood how that must have made Lila feel, at the same time, anger twisted in his gut. Obviously her trust didn't go too far if she had believed Jennifer's snide remarks. She'd run away from the restaurant, and while she had clearly arrived on his doorstep to talk about what happened, she hadn't given him any chance to explain. She'd just turned around and drove off.

He cursed again, the invectives rolling off his tongue so forcefully he almost bit off the tip. He had left so many messages on her machine he'd filled up the tape. She hadn't returned his calls. He'd written his feelings in the snow, but though he was certain she was home by now, she still hadn't picked up the phone to talk to him.

Tom tossed and turned beneath the covers, punching his pillow to ease his growing anger. He was mad at Lila, mad at Jennifer and Wendi, and mad at himself. He was even mad at Emma because, if she'd stayed home, she could have been a witness to what really went on. Not that he should have to defend himself. He punched the pillow again.

"Lila! Damn it, just call me!"

The phone mocked him with its silence. His fingers itched to dial her number again, but he resisted. He had made a fool out of himself already; he didn't need to compound the error by trying her number again. If she didn't answer, he couldn't leave a message anyway, and if she did pick up the phone....

What could he say? He had said it all with each message he'd left. He'd even written it in the snow, for God's sake. What more did the woman want?

"What does any woman want?" he asked irately to the

empty room. "I told her I loved her, damn it! Shouldn't that be enough?"

Obviously, Lila didn't think so.

Sunday passed in blessed silence. Lila didn't call or go to see Tom, and she was proud of herself for resisting the temptation. Unplugging the phone had helped.

Work on Monday was a hectic scramble, just as Lila had expected. Both she and Darren were up to their eyebrows in paperwork and meetings that had been rescheduled because of the snow. The busier she was, the better Lila felt. Throwing herself into her work left little time for anything else. That her phone kept ringing with important calls meant she couldn't use it to call anyone on personal business.

"Cleopatra wasn't the only queen of denial, honey," Darren said to her when she had refused even to break for lunch. "Working yourself to death isn't going to change what happened."

Lila gave him a steely glare. "Please let me handle this my way."

He had shrugged, clearly hurt by her rough manner. "Fine. I was only trying to help."

Nothing would help. Nothing but time, work, and maybe a few more pots of Earl Grey and a whole library of Stephen King. Lila left work later than usual, but that was all right. She had already called Rivka and told her she wouldn't be at the gallery meeting that night. Rivka, to Lila's surprise, hadn't complained.

"I understand." Rivka sounded surprisingly calm, considering the way she'd been carrying on. "We've got it all under control, Lila-love. But promise me you'll come over tomorrow night to talk about our costumes. Promise."

Lila had promised, both relieved and surprised her sister had accepted her absence from the meeting. With the gallery opening in a little over a week, her sister was in a state of slow emotional boil. Nothing Rivka could have said would have convinced Lila to go to that meeting, however. Not if she had to face Tom.

She might be taking the coward's way out, but she just didn't feel ready to see him. When she did confront him, if she ever did, she wanted to be calm. Now the pain was still raw in her heart, and she needed time for her wounds to at least scab over.

She swung by the mall on her way home, picked up some groceries, and visited the bookstore. Though her credit card practically shrieked at the overload, she treated herself to some premium ice cream and a sack of horror paperbacks. Not King, but they'd have to do.

The porch light was on when she got home so there were no shadows to hide the figure sitting on the swing. Lila pretended not to see him while she unloaded her bags from the car. When she sat the paper sacks down in order to fit her key in the lock, he stepped up.

"Why didn't you come to the meeting tonight?" Tom's voice was just this side of unfriendly.

Lila finally got the stubborn key to slide into its fittings and concentrated on opening the door. She picked up her purchases and laid them inside. She kicked the doorframe several times to clear the snow from her shoes and prepared to step inside. She hadn't answered him.

"Lila." Tom's voice was low and angry now. "Don't ignore me."

She stopped halfway through the front door and turned

to look at him. "I need some time."

"The gallery opening is in less than two weeks." He got off the porch swing. "Your sister is counting on you. I can't believe you would let your sister down just to hurt me."

She sucked in her breath at his audacity. "Don't be so vain, Tom. I didn't do it to hurt you. You can't hurt someone who doesn't care about you, remember?"

In an instant, he had grabbed her arm before she could slip inside and slam the door. His fingers hurt, even through her bulky coat. Lila yanked her arm away.

"Lila, I love you." He made no second attempt to touch her.

She laughed, the sound harsh and mocking. To her shame, she felt the hot sting of tears against her lashes, but she refused to let them slide down her cheeks. Lila lifted her chin, willing her lips not to tremble as she spoke. "So you said."

"I didn't lie."

"I don't need you to do me any favors." Her efforts at keeping the tears at bay were defeated. The shame of him seeing her cry only made her angrier. "I'm not your charity case, Tom!"

"Don't I even get a chance? Have you written me off, just like that? I don't even get the chance to tell you the truth?"

Lila gritted her teeth before she spoke. "I don't need to hear your truth. I know what it is. I've known all along. I just let your pretty face persuade me differently, that's all."

His face blanched. Her words had struck home. At the sight of his eyes, flickering with hurt, Lila wanted to call her words back. But she couldn't. That was the problem with words. You couldn't ever take them back.

"I love you, Lila." The anger was leached from his voice. "I won't say it again."

"Good," she whispered. "Because I don't think I could stand to hear you say it."

Without looking at him again, for to see his face would only weaken her, Lila stepped inside the door.

"Why?" She thought she heard tears in his voice and pretended she didn't. She didn't want to think she might have made him weep. "Why?"

"Because men like you don't date women like me. It doesn't happen, Tom. It can't. We have nothing in common. I was stupid to think it might work. Good-bye."

Her heart ached, but she shut the door behind her and leaned against it when all at once she thought she might fall. She waited for him to knock. He did not. Instead, Lila heard the sound of his feet crunching through the snow, down the porch steps, and away. Then she could hear nothing at all.

CHAPTER 10

With only a week left before the gallery opening, and her baby sister in a romantic crisis, Rivka Delaney was showing remarkable restraint. So Lila thought, anyway, watching Rivka preen in front of the floor-length mirror. She and her sister were trying on their costumes in Rivka and Mickey's bedroom.

Rivka, thus far, had not asked about Tom, for which Lila was extremely grateful. Though she knew Rivka would listen sympathetically, the pain was still too fierce, too fresh to discuss. Lila wanted to curl up and lick her wounds in private. It was the way she had always been and Rivka knew it. When Lila discovered she could laugh about Tom, whether or not the humor she found in the situation was genuine, then she would talk about him with her sister. Not before.

Nor had Rivka made any mention about the food for the party, her problems with the printer, or any of the other innumerable last-minute qualms Lila knew her sister had to be feeling. Instead, Rivka had tried on a dozen different costumes, all on loan from the costume shop and due back by this afternoon. She had finally decided on going to her party as Marie Antoinette because, as she had so dryly put it, if she was going to lose her head over this opening, she wanted to be dressed appropriately. Mick, she had explained, would be going as the little dog the French queen had been rumored to keep beneath her skirts.

"Gorgeous." Lila meant it.

Her sister looked breathtaking, as always. The dress suited her to perfection, capturing Rivka's artistic nature, innate sensuality, and vivacious nature all in one elaborate package. An extremely expensive package, too, Lila noted, looking at the price list that had come with the costumes Rivka was trying on.

"Not too cutesy?"

Resplendent in hoop skirt, powdered wig, and beauty mark, Rivka was fretting. She pressed her palms to the gown's bust and pushed her already straining bosom to new heights of plumpness. She pranced in front of the mirror, then curtseyed. To someone who didn't know her, Rivka would look the very epitome of vanity. Lila, however, knew her sister didn't really care how she looked. She never had. Rivka was nervous about the gallery opening, and the new series of paintings she would be revealing. Her moaning and complaining about her costume was just her way of pretending she wasn't afraid of all the other stuff.

"Not as cutesy as Little Bo Peep." Lila compared Rivka's elaborate, flattering costume to the one she herself planned on wearing. With its white-frilled pantaloons, blue pinafore, and stuffed sheep, she was going to look about ten years old. It was better than the costume her sister had wanted her to wear, however. No matter how desperate she might be to attract attention, Lila thought with distaste, she would never, ever go anywhere dressed as Lady Godiva.

"Oy, Bo Peep!" Rivka grimaced. "But if it makes you happy...."

"It does," Lila said firmly. "Besides, I got a great discount because the Miss Muffet costume I wanted didn't come in on time."

Rivka rolled her eyes as she examined the intricate beadwork on her skirt. She flicked her fan open and tossed it on the bed with an agonized groan. She slouched, straightened and turned to see the side view.

"I don't look creative enough. Everyone's going to expect me, the artist, to be in some great costume I made myself, and I just couldn't do it, Lila!"

Lila kissed Rivka's white-powdered cheek. "You'll knock them all out of their shoes."

"I need to knock the money out of their wallets." Rivka stopped pacing. "Help me get out of this thing, Lila-love, please."

"You know this is going to be the greatest party Harrisburg has ever seen." Lila began unhooking the myriad of tiny hooks-and-eyes that closed the back of Rivka's gown. "You don't need to worry so much."

"I know." Rivka wriggled out of the gown. "How can it not? I've got Martin setting it up, you and Tom handling the rest of it...."

Rivka's pause told Lila her sister expected an answer, but she made sure to be noncommittal. "Yes. The Foxfire has great food. I'm sure the catering will be excellent."

"That's not what I meant, and you know it." Rivka turned to Lila and searched her sister's eyes. "What happened with you two, Lila?"

Lila looked away uncomfortably. "Nothing. Things just didn't work out, that's all. No big deal."

"When my sister walks around looking like '"The Scream," it's not no big deal."

Lila smiled faintly at Rivka's comparison of her to the famous painting. She supposed that, at times, over the past five days she probably had looked like the elongated, screaming face in Munsch's painting. Lord knew she had certainly felt like it.

Lila forced lightness into her tone. "You know how handsome men are. They might say they want a woman with a brain, but they don't mean it. Not unless the brain comes in a size-34D, blonde-haired package."

Rivka frowned. "Hello! Lila? Are we talking about the same Tom Caine?"

Lila busied herself with arranging her sister's ornate costume on its hanger. She didn't want to talk about this with Rivka or with anyone. The less she talked about him, the less she had to think about him. It was going to be bad enough seeing him at the opening, but there was no way to avoid it. She couldn't let her sister down by not showing up, and she had no hopes Tom would decide not to come.

"Let it go, Riv."

Rivka took Lila by the shoulders until they faced each other. "No."

Lila wanted to throw off her sister's grasp, to shout and run away, but she could not. Rivka's jaw was set firmly, but her blue eyes were sad. At the compassion so clear in her sister's face, Lila wanted to cry.

"It was like William all over again." Lila was not surprised to find the tears welling in her eyes. It seemed that no matter how many she shed, she always had more.

"No." Rivka urged Lila to the king-size bed and sat

beside her with one arm over her sister's shoulder. "No, Lila-love, Tom isn't like William."

"What do you know?" Lila hadn't wanted to talk to Rivka about Tom, but at least she had expected her sister's sympathy.

Rivka's words weren't sympathetic. "Tom is only like William because you wanted him to be. That's what I know."

For a moment, Lila just stared at her sister in shock. Had she really said those words? Rivka, Lila's staunchest supporter, was taking Tom's side in this? Lila's mouth worked, but she could not speak. Scalding tears slid, ignored, down her face.

"Just because William hurt you doesn't mean all men will." Rivka rubbed Lila's shoulder. "Whatever Tom did, I bet you didn't even give him a chance."

Now Lila recoiled from her sister's touch. It seemed as though she could not breathe, could not see, could not do anything but listen to Rivka as she spat out more and more hateful words. Lila's bones were melting beneath her flesh, her heart was shredding itself upon the shards of her dignity, and still Rivka spoke.

"I know you, Lila. You love him. I saw it in your eyes when you looked at him and in your smile. It was in your voice when you spoke." Rivka's voice was so hard, so cold. Lila wanted to block it out, but Rivka held her hands so she could not. "And I saw the same thing in his face. Tom loves you. I never saw a man light up so much as he did when you walked in the room. When I told him you weren't coming to that last meeting, I thought he was going to faint, Lila, that's how bad he looked. Tom Caine almost wept in front of me because I told him you weren't coming to a stupid meeting."

"You don't know." Lila forced the words through

parched lips. "You don't know what happened."

"I don't have to know. I know you're afraid. William was a dirty, lying jerk, and I wish you wouldn't even grant him the dignity of having hurt you, but I understand." Rivka squeezed Lila's shoulder gently.

"You and Mick—" Lila began, desperate to turn the conversation away from herself.

"Just because I've been lucky enough to find my Mickey doesn't mean I can't remember how it was to be hurt!" Rivka knelt beside Lila, who had somehow slid from the bed to crouch on the floor. "Lila, my sister, I hurt a thousand times watching you let the things William said wear away your self-confidence. I hurt when you hurt."

Lila shook her head blindly. "The woman in the restaurant called me his charity case. It was just like William all over again. I was stupid to think a man like Tom would ever look at me twice, much less fall in love with me. And even if he did think he loved me, it's better this way. Better it ends now, when I can handle it, than years from now when he decides he wants a woman like Jennifer on his arm and not someone like me."

"Now when you can handle it?" Rivka didn't sound convinced. "You've lost weight, Lila, and you've got circles under your eyes. You aren't handling it at all."

Lila wiped her face. "I could be handling it, if you'd just leave me alone about it. I'll get over him."

Rivka moved away, disdain on her perfect features. "You let a man who wasn't worth the ground you spit on take away what I've always admired about you. William made you Lila forever. You're not bold at all."

Rivka left the room. Lila stared after her until the tears dried on her cheeks. The words her sister had said stung worse than a swarm of bees, but Lila no longer felt boneless and weak. She felt angry and not at Rivka. At William, who had made her sister ashamed of her. And at herself, for letting him.

Emma was singing in the shower. Her enthusiastic, off-tune words floated down the hall into Tom's bedroom, where he was trying—without success—to sleep. He gritted his teeth against her happiness and buried his face in the pillow.

He could not begrudge his niece her joy. If only she wasn't so vocal about it! Tom had never heard more love songs in his life than in the past week. Emma, it seemed, was an incurable romantic. She quoted Romeo and Juliet over breakfast. She made up terrible but heartfelt poetry and read it aloud to him in an awful Elizabethan accent, and expected him to give his true opinion about it. She had even invited Michel to dinner at the house and baked him a heart-shaped meatloaf. The girl was crazy. He listened to Emma's song crescendo into an almost unbearable, deliriously love-struck trilling.

Months ago, Emma's behavior would have made him laugh. A week ago, he'd probably have been singing right along with her. Since Lila had shut him out of her life, Tom had never felt less like listening to the wonder and beauty of love as seen by his freckle-faced niece.

He had fired both Jennifer and Wendi, despite their threats of claiming sexual harassment. He'd risk it, he'd told them. They'd get their last paychecks in the mail, don't bother coming in to The Foxfire, good-bye and I hope not to see you later.

None of that could bring Lila back. After the confrontation on her porch, he had itched to dial her number a thousand times, but never had. He had driven past her house, but did not stop. He wanted to see her so badly he ached, but what could he do? She didn't want to see him. She didn't trust him. She didn't love him.

But ah, God! He still loved her! Every note of music on the radio, every star shining in his window while he tossed, sleepless in his bed...they all reminded him of her. Her eyes, her smile, the sound of his name coming from her lips. Everything, everything was Lila, and he could do nothing to stop himself from thinking of her.

He had written a dozen letters and thrown them all away. He didn't have any talent with words, not even Emma's poor one for poetry. Tom was a man who used action to show how he felt. If he spoke, it was from the heart. And wasn't that what had gotten him into so much trouble? Speaking from the heart?

Tom heard the shower shut off. Emma, still singing, came down the hall and paused outside his door. He willed her to go away, but the sound of her hesitant tapping on his door told him his wish had been ignored.

"Boss?"

"I'm awake."

A thin sliver of light pierced the blackness of his room. Emma stood outlined in the doorway, her figure bulky in a terrycloth robe and thick towel swathed around her head. She stepped through the doorway.

"It's only seven o'clock on a Saturday night. Don't you feel well?"

"Just tired." He bit out the words like he was chewing jerky. "I've had a rough week."

"You haven't even been out this week." Emma's tone was slightly accusing. She flicked on the light switch, which made him groan and fling his arm across his eyes. "You look like hell."

"Gee, thanks." Tom slid up in the bed until he rested against the headboard. "Any other personal criticism you'd like to leave with me? I'm all up for it."

Emma sat on the edge of the bed. "What happened with Lila?"

Tom ran his hand through his hair. Then he scrubbed his face with his hands, and the stubble scratched his fingers. He hadn't shaved for three days, or showered, or done much of anything but lay in bed. He only hoped The Foxfire would still be standing by the time he got back to work.

"'This isn't like you. I'm worried about you."

"I've never been in love before." As he said the words, he felt some of the burden he'd been feeling lift. No wonder women talked to their girlfriends. It made everything seem bearable.

"Oh, boss." Emma made a sympathetic noise.

"She thinks she's not pretty enough. I tried to tell her that to me she was beautiful. She didn't believe me. I tried telling her it wasn't her face I loved anyway, but she didn't believe that either. I couldn't win, Em. I just couldn't win."

"It's the one time in your life your face hasn't gotten you what you wanted." Emma's nonchalant reply wasn't what he wanted to hear.

Tom's back stiffened. "Thanks."

"I'm being honest." Emma shrugged. "You've had it real good your whole life, boss. Women have just fallen all over you. You've never had to work at anything because no one ever turned you down."

"What's that supposed to mean?" Now he realized why

men didn't talk about these things with their guy friends. Blunt, brutal honesty. It was a real bitch.

"I heard the whole story about last Saturday night from Donna at The Foxfire." Emma let out a low whistle. "Lila got double-teamed by two pros—Jen and Wendi. It would take a woman with nerves of steel not to buckle under that."

"But I never said she was my charity case! I told her those women were nothing! I told her how I felt about her!"

Emma snorted. "All you men. You think your words are enough. What did you do to show her?"

"She didn't want to listen to me. She closed the door in my face."

"Did you knock?"

He had not, but he didn't want to say so. "I don't play games, Emma!"

His niece scowled and crossed her arms at him. "And my guess is Lila doesn't either. She's not playing hard to get."

"Well, what is she doing?"

"I don't know." Emma shrugged. "But if you really love her, I don't think you'd have given up so easily."

"I didn't give up. I shouldn't have to fight for her to listen to me." Tom thumped his head on the headboard.

Emma rolled her eyes. "That's what love is all about. Fighting to keep what you want. Fighting to keep the one you love from harm. Fighting to make your pig-headed lover see the truth if that's what you need to do!"

"Are you calling me pig-headed?"

"I think you must both be stubborn idiots if you're letting two bimbos who don't know when to keep their mouths shut come between you."

"What are you saying?" Tom was bewildered at how his

younger niece had managed to learn so much about love while he had remained clueless.

Emma made a noise of long-suffering patience. "I'm saying that if you love her, you shouldn't let her shut you out. If she loves you, she'll listen. If she doesn't, then at least you'll know. Either way, it'll be better than hibernating in here forever."

"You harder on me than your mother ever was."

Emma shrugged. "Learned from the best, I guess."

Tom allowed a ghost of a smile to touch his lips. "Maybe I should hire a skywriter. Or take out an ad in the paper."

"Maybe. Or maybe you should just tell her you understand how she feels. Instead of trying so hard to make her believe you think she's great, try a little harder to understand why she doesn't." Emma grinned. "That's what we women want, boss—someone to understand us."

"She dated a guy who made her feel ugly." Tom briefly told Emma the story of William and his "favor."

Emma groaned. "No wonder she got so upset! I'm surprised she even went out with you at all, looking the way you do."

"Can we forget about my face for a minute?"

"Sure. Short of plastic surgery, it's not going to change anyway."

Tom sighed. "So what do I do now? If she won't take my calls, I mean."

"You do have a certain event coming up." Emma gave him a sly glance. "It might be the perfect place to show Lila—and the world—what she means to you."

Tom shook his head. "Emma, you scare me."

"Genius always scares those who don't understand it," Emma replied serenely, getting off the bed and going to the door.

"I'll be taking a huge chance," he called after her.

"That's what love is all about." Emma stopped in the doorway. "Taking chances."

"I thought you said it was about fighting."

"Who am I, Dr. Ruth?" Then she was out the door and he was left to ponder all she'd said.

Had he taken Lila's trust in him for granted? Had he just assumed she would believe him, just because no one had ever not believed in him before? Possibly. He had never been in love before, and, as Emma had said, had never had to work for anything before. He had assumed Lila would hear his words and know the depth of his sincerity, when in reality, had he not mouthed similar phrases in the past without meaning them? True, he'd never said he'd loved anyone before, but Lila couldn't know that.

Yes, she ought to have trusted him. But he should have made sure she had no doubts. It was up to him to make her see he couldn't live without her. And more importantly, that Lila couldn't live without him.

The shoebox wasn't heavy, though it was stuffed to overflowing. Lila took it down from the depths of her closet and blew a layer of dust off the top. The cardboard was faded, the writing on it nearly illegible, but she knew what it said—Lila's Stuff.

Not the most elegant way to describe the mementos of her romantic life, but accurate. Lila curled up on the bed and lifted the lid. The contents weren't arranged in any sort of order, but she didn't mind. She had no plans for the evening.

She sifted through the items in the box and matched

pieces that went together. When she was done, she was left with what looked like piles of paper. What she really had was a chronology of her life as a woman.

Her first boyfriend, Brett. At seventeen, he'd been handsome and funny, a soccer player for the school team. Cocky.He'd told her he loved her while standing on the front porch of her parent's house and risked curfew to steal a few extra kisses. He'd probably said the words to try and get her into bed. That gave her a smile. His plan had failed. She caressed the picture of the two of them at the prom. She'd worn a pink dress and ballerina slippers so she wouldn't be taller than him.

Another prom picture. She was a year older, thinner, wearing an emerald green gown. Her second high-school love, Shawn, beamed from the photo with his arms around her waist. He'd been in the band, not an athlete, and he didn't have Brett's attitude. Though their breakup had been bitter, they had managed to salvage their friendship after a few years.

College photos came—a slew of photos and letters from her years at school. A love poem from a secret admirer she had later discovered to be the most popular boy in her dorm. They'd dated once or twice, but no more than that. And why? Because Lila had started dating a guy in her theater elective. What was his name? Tobin. He hadn't been handsome. He'd been skinny, dark-haired, and a chain-smoker. Yet, something about him had been so exciting....

All the men in her life. Lila riffled through the piles she had made. Some had hurt her, some she had hurt. Others had done neither. And what did that tell her now?

She sure wasn't dumb; she'd always known that. Yet, she had allowed William to make her feel that way. She wasn't ugly either, though he had made her feel that way, too. Lila felt the slow burn of anger begin again in her belly. All those young men in her life, and only one had ever made her feel unworthy of being loved.

She found the only photo of William she had. The surprise photo had been taken at her office holiday party. It was the only photo she had of William because he had always refused to allow her to capture him on film. At the time, she had thought it was because he wanted nothing to show just how pathetically unattractive his girlfriend really was. Looking at the photo now, however, Lila saw a different truth.

She wore a velvet gown of royal blue, her hair tied up in a complicated swirl of curls that William had complained made her look too fussy. She was holding onto William's arm, laughing and looking up at him. He wasn't even smiling. Lila was radiant, her cheeks flushed from laughing and her eyes asparkle. She looked beautiful, and William looked....

"Not as handsome as I remember." Lila touched the tiny figures in the picture. "I guess nobody ever told you that you can catch more flies with honey than with vinegar, Willy."

He'd hated being called Willy, or Will, or even Billy. Staid, arrogant, full-of-himself William. Lila crumpled the picture with a sudden twist of her fingers and stared at the wad a moment. Smoothing the picture carefully, she placed it back in the box with the others. She might need to look at it again, sometime.

William had been wrong about her. He had not been doing Lila a favor. It had been the other way around. Lila had done William a favor by letting him in her life. She had made him laugh once or twice, and it was probably the only time in his life he'd ever let himself go so wild.

All at once, as if the sun had come out from behind the clouds, Lila felt the weight of William's betrayal fall away from her. It didn't matter any more what he thought. What Tom had told her was true. You can't hurt someone who doesn't care about you. William couldn't hurt her anymore because she didn't care about him.

"I love Tom." The words filled her with a bubble of joy that tickled her insides.

So what if women were falling all over him? He had chosen to be with her, hadn't he? Didn't that say anything?

"I love Tom Caine. I love him!"

She was ashamed she had let Jennifer's cruel words pierce her. The blonde hostess meant nothing to Lila, and nothing she said ever again could possibly bother her. Lila was also ashamed she had not trusted Tom. Because Tom wasn't William.

Lila put the box back from where she had taken it and relegated it once more to the depths of her closet. She didn't need to see anything in there anymore. Though the memories it held would always be pleasant, none of those romances could compare to what she felt for the tall man with hazel eyes whom she'd met at her sister's art showing. The joys and sorrows of all those past relationships had shaped her into the woman she was, true, but what she had shared with Tom had shown her the woman she was going to become.

It was like growing up all over again. Struggling through the angst of adolescence, trying to find herself. Trying to see herself as others saw her, whether their opinions were based on her face, her soul, or where she lived and what sort of car she drove.

It didn't matter how everyone else saw her now. All that

mattered was how she saw herself. The reflection she saw in Tom's eyes was how she wanted to be.

She would tell him that, too, and hope she was not too late. She would apologize for not trusting him. She would make things right.

Feeling suddenly empowered, Lila plucked a wrench from her toolbox and headed for the basement. Making things right with Tom was important, yes, but first she had to do something else, something for herself. It was time for her to fix that blasted furnace.

CHAPTER 11

TOM COULDN'T BELIEVE the week had flown by so fast. The grand opening of The Gallery on Second was tomorrow night. Not only did he not have a costume prepared, he had no idea of how he was going to prove to Lila he really loved her.

He wished he could use his lack of interest in work as proof of his change in priorities, but that hardly seemed enough. Tonight was the third night this week he'd left the restaurant early, something he rarely did even though Frank Philips was a top-notch manager. Tom liked to mingle with the customers. He had worked hard to make The Foxfire the success it had become, and nothing gave him more satisfaction than finishing the night knowing all had gone well. Since the blowup with Lila, however, he found he couldn't care less whether the new appetizers were well-received, or anything else. Only about Lila.

Now he was sitting at the bar in Malley's Pub, sucking down a pint of warm beer and waiting to hear Mick's band play. The Roving Ramblers had gone through one set already, their lively mix of traditional Celtic music and

Cajun Zydeco surprisingly well-blended. They had taken a break, amid groans of protest from the people in the packed bar. The Ramblers were a huge draw for Malley's, and ordinarily Tom would have considered hitting Mick up to play a night or two at The Foxfire. Tonight, though, he just didn't feel like talking shop. He only wanted to think about Lila.

His suggestions about a skywriter and an ad in the newspaper didn't seem so crazy now. They seemed easier than the alternative, which was to talk to her face-to-face. Tom hadn't wanted to admit it to Emma, but the thought of confronting Lila scared him. Emma had been right about him never having to work for anything before. Women had always flocked around him like seagulls fighting over a French fry. He'd never had to face rejection. Then again, he'd never cared so much about anyone before.

"Our next set's up in five, Tom." Pint of Guinness in hand, Mick appeared beside him at the bar. Rivka's husband winked and clapped Tom on the shoulder. "Next round's on me. Sure and you look like you be needin' it. I've seen happier faces on a flea-bit dog."

Tom smiled half-heartedly. "Can't you talk some sense into your sister-in-law?"

"Ah, and if I could sing the birdies down from the trees, would you be after havin' me do that as well?" Clearly Mick had no illusions about his ability to affect Lila. "'Tis my Rivka you need to be talkin' to."

Tom tossed back the last half of his pint. "She won't talk to me. Says it's not her place."

"Now that would be a first." Mick shook his head and grinned. "When my Rivka leaves her pretty nose out of her sister's business—"

"What about my nose?" Rivka appeared suddenly

beside him. Mick smiled shamefacedly and kissed her. "The rest of the boys are waiting for you, Mickey."

Mick took the pointed hint and tipped an imaginary hat toward Tom. Rivka watched her black-haired husband weave his way through the crowd to the small stage area and sighed. She turned and signaled to the bartender.

"I'll have a white wine." She pointed to Tom. "He's paying."

Obligingly, Tom pulled out his wallet and paid for her drink. They sat in mutual silence for a few minutes. From behind them, The Roving Ramblers began their next set. Mick had forsaken his guitar for a set of uillean pipes, and the haunting melody seemed to squeeze Tom's throat until he could hardly breathe.

"This is one of my favorites," Rivka remarked off-handedly. "It's so sad, though. Don't you just feel like crying?"

Tom looked at her sternly. "Don't play games with me, Rivka. You said you weren't going to talk to me about Lila, so I haven't said anything. Yes, I'm upset about losing her, but what can I do? I've wracked my brains to think of a way to prove I love her, and I just can't come up with one. It really burns me up that she didn't just trust me."

Rivka clicked her tongue against her teeth. "You know about William, of course."

Tom growled and finished the rest of his pint. "I'd like to punch that bastard right in the face. It's all his fault."

Rivka rolled her eyes and looked so much like Lila his heart hurt again. "It's not William's fault, Tom. It's yours, and Lila's, too. Poor Billy is only an excuse."

Without asking, the bartender took Tom's mug and refilled it. Tom stared at the thick, creamy head of foam atop the dark brew. He knew Rivka was right. It was just easier to blame things on William Darcy.

"So what can I do about it?"

Rivka rolled her eyes again and added a sigh so deep it had to have come from her toes. "Men!"

"What?" Tom's defenses rose. "Rivka, I feel bad enough, so if you're going to man bash...."

"I'm not going to bash anyone." Rivka finished the last of her wine. She stood up and tugged his shoulder. "C'mon."

He looked at her warily. The Roving Ramblers weren't even close to finishing their gig. Rivka's grin made him nervous.

Suspicion filled him. "What do you want?"

"Come with me to the Gallery. To the studio. I want to paint you."

"Oh, no." Tom shook his head. "No way."

She frowned. "C'mon. You need this."

"I need this?"

"Yeah. You need this."

"Like I need a hole in my head." Tom grumbled, but he got off the stool. Rivka had a way about her that didn't make her easy to deny. For one moment, Tom both envied and pitied Mick Delaney, who had made this wacky woman his wife.

"I'll give you a hole in your head if you don't move your butt." Rivka laughed. "C'mon, Tom, I need another X-Man."

Even though he was already on his feet and following her out of the bar, Tom stopped. "The X-Men again. What am I, just a face?"

Rivka didn't wait for him, instead pushing open the door to the parking lot. She called over her shoulder to him. "God gives us certain things in life. It's stupid to deny them."

Like he was being sucked along in the wake of an avalanche, Tom followed her to the lot. The frigid night air swept away some of the cobwebs he'd been allowing to cover him. He couldn't believe he was actually going along with this.

The drive to The Gallery on Second was too short. He groaned to himself as he followed Rivka inside and to the small studio in the back. He watched as she flicked on lights and busied herself with pots of paint, brushes, and canvas.

"Rivka, I really don't think I want to do this. I don't see the point."

Rivka turned toward him, no longer teasing. "The point is it will make you feel better."

He barked out something that was supposed to be a laugh, but didn't quite make it. "This whole issue with Lila is because she says I'm too good looking to fall in love with her. How can having my portrait painted make me feel any better about that? Are you going to show me with warts or something? A hunchback?"

Rivka was busy scraping her short curls away from her face and pinning them. "You don't have any warts. And your back looks fine to me."

"I wish I did have warts! Or a whole bunch of scars."

"Chicks dig scars." Rivka pointed. "Sit."

Despite his misgivings, he sat. Stiff. Like a board. He couldn't remember ever feeling so self-conscious. He'd never had his picture painted before, and he wasn't sure what to expect. Something to do with berets maybe, or Rivka standing in front of him holding up her thumb. French accents. Oh, hell, what did he know about painting?

Rivka's silence didn't make things any more comfortable. She worked in silence, unbroken except for the scratch of her brush against the canvas. Her pretty face was furrowed in concentration, and he had time to study her.

"Lila says you're the pretty one and she's the smart one."

He wanted to break the silence with something, even lame conversation. "Some kind of family joke?"

"Yeah. Our parents refused to compare us, so we had to do it for ourselves."

"So why did Lila get the short end of the stick?" The whole idea suddenly irritated him. He still wanted to lay blame, to ease the ache inside him.

Rivka bit her lip and studied her work. "What, you think being pretty is better than being smart? I always thought I got the short end."

Agreeing with her would make him sound exactly like the sort of man Lila thought he was. "I just meant that I don't think Lila isn't pretty."

Rivka looked up from her painting to stare at him seriously. "She's damn gorgeous."

Taken aback by the force of her words, Tom shifted on his chair. "Well, yeah. But she doesn't think so. And I want to know why."

Rivka sighed. "Because of us comparing ourselves. Because of William Darcy. Because of women like your sad excuse for a hostess. Why, why, why? Who ever feels totally comfortable with the way they look, Tom? Bad Billy was the biggest part of why my Lila-love shut herself away, but he's just one piece."

"So what can I do?" Tom slammed his fists down on his thighs. "I love her, Rivka!"

He got up from the chair, not caring that he might be ruining her portrait. He felt the embarrassing acid sting of tears, and he didn't want to cry in front of Lila's sister. Instead, he stalked the length of the tiny studio and back. If only he could run and run, until all of this just melted away. Until he melted away and didn't have to think about it any more.

"I don't know, honey." Thankfully she didn't try and hug him or anything like that. He heard the faint scritch scratch of her brush, ever moving, on the picture. "I wish I could wave my magic wand and turn it all to gold, but right now it's all just a big pile of dog doo. And frankly, gold dog doo isn't much better than the regular kind."

Surprisingly, Tom felt a chuckle bubbling in his chest. It had escaped his throat before he knew it and sounded loud in the tiny space. He turned back to the woman still busy at her canvas. Tendrils of hair had come loose around her face and gave her a wild appearance. Paint had smeared one cheek. She looked every bit as eccentric as she liked people to believe she was.

"You are such a kook."

She paused, looking at him with one raised brow that he recognized as the patented Lazin sisters glare. "Moi?"

Tom sighed and sat back down so she could paint him without so much effort. "I guess I'm the kook. The jerk, the numbskull, whatever. And I'd gladly tell Lila that, but...."

"But she won't see you." Rivka nodded. "I know. She's like that. Stubborn. It's a family trait. But that won't matter because you'll both be at the opening of the gallery and so will he."

"He? You mean Darcy?"

"I invited him to the opening."

"You did what?" Shocked, Tom glared at her.

Rivka smiled. "Down, boy. Relax. It'll be all right."

He couldn't believe Rivka would subject her sister to seeing the man who had hurt her so badly. He figured Lila would be tense enough about seeing him there, much less her old boyfriend. "Why?" It had become obvious Rivka wasn't going to explain herself.

"Because it's time Lila-love got over him. And besides, I

have some information that's going to help you a lot."

"You do?"

Rivka grinned wickedly. Whatever she had up her sleeve was going to be good. "Our Bad Billy isn't keeping his marriage vows."

Tom looked at her cautiously. "What?"

Rivka kept painting—her arms moving faster as she applied paint with both hands. "He's cheating on his wife."

"How do you know this?"

"I've seen them together, him and his fling." Rivka frowned, adding a dab of paint here and another there. "Harrisburg's a pretty small town, Tom. Word gets around."

"So what does this have to do with me and Lila?"

"If you were planning on doing anything for Lila tomorrow night...."

"Yes?" What she left unspoken intrigued him.

Rivka shrugged too casually. "I just thought I'd let you know William is going to be there, that's all. In case you had some things you wanted to tell him. Or make him tell her. Or something."

An idea had begun forming in Tom's head, and he grinned. When Rivka returned the smile, he knew he was thinking exactly what she wanted him to. He winked at her. "Thanks, Rivka. I think I'd like to meet that guy."

"I thought you might."

"So much for staying out of your sister's business."

Rivka gave him a look of disdain. "I never said I was staying out of her business. Besides, she's my sister. Her business is my business. I want her to be happy, Tom."

She paused. "She was happy with you."

"She couldn't have been too happy." Some of his sour mood returned. "Not if she turned me away so fast for something I didn't even say or do."

"I know my sister. You made her happy. She was just too stupid to see she had a good thing going."

"Thanks," Tom said grudgingly. "I appreciate it."

"Then sit down and be quiet so I can paint." Rivka pointed again, and Tom found he had no choice but to do as she said.

Lila wasn't much of a seamstress. She hadn't inherited any of her sister's talents for creation, not in painting or writing or cooking, and most definitely not in sewing. Still, she had withstood pricked fingers, broken needles, and snapped threads to make this costume for tomorrow night's opening. She shook out the folds of shimmering metallic material. The question was...would it be worth it?

She'd had the good fortune to find the pattern tucked in the clearance box at the fabric store. It must have been left over from Halloween and had been marked down to the ridiculously low price of twenty-five cents. Even if it had been twenty-five dollars, however, Lila would have bought it.

Taking a cue from something Darren had said to her, Lila had decided to forgo the cute Little Bo Peep costume. She'd never been a fan of lamb. She returned the costume to the store, using the balance of her deposit to buy the wig she now pulled over her own hair. It fell in sleek dark lines to her shoulders and across her forehead. Nestled into the black strands was a headpiece of gold in the shape of a snake.

"Cleopatra ain't the only queen of denial." Staring at her reflection, Lila laughed. "Not bad."

Shimmying out of her comfortable sweatsuit, she pulled

on the dress she had labored over for the past three nights. Thankfully, the pattern had been simple enough for even her inadequate skills, though the metallic cloth had been a real pain to work with. She shook her shoulders until the gown fell into graceful folds over her body and down to her feet.

Next came the padded shoulder pieces, linked together with tiny snakes she had also been fortunate enough to find in the bargain bin. This had been the most difficult part of the costume, requiring hand-sewn braiding and decorations. She'd nearly hot-glued her fingers together, but the results looked good.

Lila practiced looking regal. In keeping with her vision of the legendary Egyptian beauty, she'd applied far more makeup than she usually did. A different woman stared back at her from the mirror. She outlined her eyes with dark slashes of kohl and filled in her lips with lipstick the color of blood. Now her eyes were startlingly bright blue against the black makeup, and her mouth glistened, the lips plump and inviting. She hardly knew herself.

She primped. "Not an everyday look. But it'll do."

Truthfully, she was more than pleased at how the entire costume had come together. She hardly recognized herself. That was good. The Lila who needed to confront Tom Caine needed to be a little different for tomorrow night. She needed the courage the face paint and elaborate dress would provide.

Slipping out of the dress and wig, Lila stepped back into the worn cotton sweatpants and sweatshirt she'd owned for years. Once navy blue, the suit had faded through countless washings until it was a nondescript gray. It sagged in places she didn't, but was as soft as flannel and just as comforting. The sweatsuit might not be fit for a queen, but Lila liked it anyway.

Padding into the bathroom in stocking feet, she scrubbed away the red and black marks from her face until she was once again her old self. Oddly enough, even though she no longer saw Cleopatra staring at her from above the bathroom sink, Lila still felt changed.

For the first time in what seemed forever, she really scrutinized her reflection. Her blue-ice eyes were different from her sister's by only the slightest of shades. Her mouth was thicker than Rivka's, and her nose, thinner. The dark, wild brows matched the dark tangle of curls falling to her shoulders. Her skin was slightly pinker from the scrubbing she had given it, but was rapidly fading back into the pale cream that never really tanned.

"Huh. I don't look so much like Rivka after all."

She wasn't a plainer version of her sister, as she had always thought. She was perfect version of herself. The flaws, both real and imagined, only served to make her face unique.

She shivered a little in anticipation and hugged herself. She would see Tom tomorrow night. She would show him denial was just a river in Egypt. Show him, and show herself, too.

Tom pulled his Tahoe into the space Rivka had reserved for him. Thank goodness for the parking garage. The parking lot behind The Gallery on Second was completely full. Even the space reserved for Lila was filled, which meant she was already here. At the thought, his heart thumped a little faster.

He sat for a moment in the truck. Tonight could be the

most important night of his life, and not just because he had invested a lot of money in Rivka's gallery. Tonight he was going to ask Lila Lazin to become his wife.

He had turned his brain inside out trying to think of ways to prove his love for her. Finally, Tom decided nothing could say more than the simple but elegant square-cut diamond he had in his coat pocket. The ring had been his grandmother's, and he wanted Lila to wear it. Not to prove anything. Not to fix anything. Just because he did love her and the thought of living the rest of his life without her was too horrible to contemplate.

He would ask Lila to marry him and brave whatever response she gave. Slipping the ring into the small velvet pouch he'd bought from a jeweler, he carefully secured the bag's ties around a belt loop. Then he tucked the pouch away, out of sight. Though it caused an odd bulge, he left it that way. It might garner him a few strange looks, but then again, maybe not. He was sure there would be stranger sights at the party than his bulging bellybutton.

A loud group of partygoers passed by on their way into the gallery. They were dressed as a cruise ship. The man in the center of the group wore a captain's hat with a model of an actual ship around his waist. Surrounding him were two people dressed as crazy tourists, complete with loud Hawaiian shirts and life jackets. One person was dressed as a waiter, carrying a tray of tropical drinks, while another woman carrying a clipboard was obviously the cruise director. There was even a person dressed as a lobster.

People had really gone all out for this party, just as Rivka had wanted. Tom was glad. He had long admired Rivka's works, and truly felt she deserved a showcase for her paintings. If the gallery was going to be a success, however, it needed some good publicity. It looked like she was going to get it. The mayor passed by dressed as George Washington. It was the same costume he wore to all the masked events in Harrisburg.

Tom gathered his keys and got out of the truck. The bitter wind instantly assailed his bare legs and arms, and he let out a low whistle of discomfort. Shifting his legs rapidly to keep some warmth in them, he pulled the rest of his costume from the back seat. Helmet. Sword. Shield. Finally, a laurel wreath to cover his hair. He was ready.

He had initially decided to go dressed as a lamb, after learning of Lila's costume choice of Little Bo Peep. He had even gone so far as to try the damned woolly thing on, standing in front of the mirror looking like an idiot. The suit was too small. His arms had hung out a good two inches below the sleeves, and his ankles were bare, too. The stupid, floppy headpiece hadn't even closed around his neck.

Emma, who had decided to attend the ball as Glinda the Good Witch, couldn't stop laughing. In fact, she'd laughed so hard and long Tom had threatened to drop a house on her. His suggestion had only made her howl even more.

"That was the other witch!" Emma had held her pink-sequined sides and nearly stabbed herself with her wand. "Boss, you look like a freak!"

"What am I supposed to do?" He'd paced back and forth, or wagged his tail behind him, as the rhyme would have it. "The party is in three hours. I don't have anything else to wear."

Emma, fortunately, had come through again. Rifling through the trunk in her room, she'd pulled out the costume he now wore. She'd even thrown in a couple of copper armbands from her jewelry box.

"Should I ask why you have this laying around?" Tom

grew suspicious when she handed him the leather skirt and breastplate.

"No. And don't mention it to Mom either."

Surprisingly, and luckily for Tom, whoever the costume had been meant for originally was just his size. Even the flat leather sandals with rawhide laces fit him, though the laces did pull on the hairs of his leg rather annoyingly.

"You'll get used to it." Emma blushed. Tom didn't ask any more questions.

So now here he was, dressed as Mark Antony. Another gust of winter wind swirled around his legs and chilled him in places he'd rather not have chilled. Tom needed to enter the party before he lost all sensation in his toes. Mingling with the other guests pushing through the front door, he no longer felt self-conscious. He spotted two men dressed even more skimpily than he was, both wearing little more than a pair of socks and a bunch of balloons. Green for one and purple for the other. Grapes, Tom realized.

"'Tom!" Rivka called to him in an imperious voice from across the room. She flicked open her fan. "Come here! We can't move in this gown!"

She must be using the royal "we." Tom pushed his way through the throngs of costumed revelers. Mick was nowhere in sight. Martin, however, was close at hand. His only concession to the party was a polka-dotted bow tie that lit up and twirled around. He was demonstrating the tie to a man dressed as a sailor and a beautiful woman in a red sequined gown who looked like Diana Ross. Tom nodded a greeting when he finally got close enough to speak to Rivka without shouting. "Quite the turnout."

Rivka looked pleased. "Yes, thank God. I hope there'll be enough food."

Tom grinned at her pointed remark. "Of course there will be, Your Majesty."

"Good." Rivka let out a peal of nervous laughter. "Oh, Tom, isn't this great? Everyone's here. Did you see the mayor? He came as old George, of course."

"I saw him." Tom looked around. "Where's Mick?"

"Rowf." Mick stuck his head out from beneath Rivka's voluminous skirts. A brown fur cap with long floppy ears covered his black hair. Black face paint covered his nose and ringed one eye. He waved a bone at Tom.

Tom just goggled for a moment, stunned by Mick's sudden appearance. "What are you doing under there?"

"He's my little dog." Rivka rapped Mick on the head with her fan as he tried to lick her hand. "My naughty little pooch. I take him with me to the guillotine, you know, and have his little head chopped off, too."

Tom grimaced. "Ouch."

"That's what Martin told me anyway." Rivka poked her dealer unceremoniously with her fan. "Right?"

Martin pulled his attention away from the woman in the red dress long enough to reply. "Certainly, Rivka."

"I don't believe we've met," the woman who had so captivated Martin cooed, extending one slim hand to Tom. "I'm Miss Ross, of course."

"Pleasure." Tom took the woman's hand. "Tom...I mean Mark Antony."

The woman's fingers squeezed his for a moment, her dark eyes shimmering against her caramel-colored skin. She swept a mane of curly black hair out of her eyes. "Mr. Gorgeous." She nudged the sailor.

"Have we met?"

"No, honey," Miss Ross said. "But I've heard all about you. I'm Lila's assistant, Darren Ramsey."

Martin choked rather loudly. Tom did a double-take. Miss Ross smiled, obviously pleased that her costume had fooled them.

"Is Lila here?" Tom was unable to think of any other response.

Darren waved a sequined arm around the room. "Oh, yes. She's around here someplace."

"She's supposed to be dressed as Little Bo Peep," Rivka said in disdain, every inch her royal majesty. "How bourgeois!"

"I'm going to find her."

Darren's hand on his arm stopped him. "She's not dressed as Bo Peep."

"What is she dressed as?"

"That," Miss Ross said Supremely, "is for you to find out, honey."

Tom shrugged, confused. Taking his leave of Rivka and the others, he began making his way toward the food. He wanted to make sure everything was all right since The Foxfire was doing the catering. He'd just take a quick look and be off on his mission to find Lila.

He found the buffet table groaning with food. Emma, delightfully whimsical in her frothy pink costume, was making suggestions to several hungry revelers who seemed overwhelmed by the choices. Michel, looking rigid and uncomfortable dressed as the Cowardly Lion, was overseeing the servers who stood on either side of the table.

"Looks great," Tom complimented the chef.

Emma waggled her brows at him. "So do you, boss. Look at those knees!"

"Nice costume." The man to Tom's left was dressed as Julius Caesar.

Something seemed familiar about him, though Tom

couldn't quite place it. Perhaps the man had come into the restaurant on occasion. It seemed the most likely explanation, though just where he had seen the guy before nagged at his mind. He shrugged off the feeling, certain it would come to him in time.

"Enjoy the salad." Tom indicated the man's plate. "We made it because we knew you would be coming. Fresh anchovies and everything."

The man stared blankly at him for a moment, than laughed rather insincerely. "Funny." He stuck out his hand. "William Darcy."

"Tom Caine." Tom was already shaking the man's hand before the name sank in. When he realized who he had in his grip, he had to make a conscious effort not to bear down and grind the man's bones to a pulp. This was the man who had hurt Lila.

"Nice party." A petite, platinum-blonde woman dressed predictably as Marilyn Monroe appeared beside Darcy.

He draped his arm around her shoulders. "This is Pansy, my wife."

Pansy? Tom shook the woman's hand politely. This was the woman Darcy had chosen over Lila? The petite blonde was pretty, sure, but in the same way thousands of other women are pretty. She had nothing that made her stand out from the crowd, except perhaps for her immense chest. It rose from the top of her white halter dress like twin mountain peaks. Tom bet he could rest a drink on each one, and she wouldn't spill a drop.

"This place is so...neat." Pansy paused for a long moment as though she was having trouble finding an adjective strong enough to describe her feelings. "I think I might buy one of the paintings for the rumpus room."

"Just don't buy any that are over in that room." Darcy

tweaked her nose. He pointed to the Bold Room, the room Rivka had set aside to honor Lila.

"Right." Pansy sniffed. "Like I want a picture of your ex-girlfriend in our house."

"She was hardly a girlfriend." Darcy turned to Tom, speaking with casual pride. Though he had just denied his real relationship with Lila, clearly he thought it a bragging matter to mention he had dated the artist's sister. "I dated Lila Lazin. Her sister dedicated that room over there to her."

"You know Lila?" Red rage boiled up and threatened to erupt through his fists.

"Sure." The pompous braggart appeared relaxed and somewhat talkative. Pansy had tripped off to look at the prints for sale along the far wall. "Nice enough girl, though not much to look at. And somewhat stupid as well."

"She must have been, to date you," Tom muttered through clenched teeth.

"What did you say?" Darcy seemed unable to believe his ears.

"Say." Tom clapped Darcy's shoulder suddenly, jovially, as though Darcy was his best friend in all the world. "We've met before, you know."

Darcy furrowed his brow. "I don't think so."

"Sure." Tom gave him a light punch to the upper arm. Real man-to-man bonding. "In the parking lot behind my restaurant."

A slow flush crept up Darcy's thick neck toward his face. "I'm sure I don't know what you mean."

"Of course you do." Tom's fingers became talons in Darcy's flesh. "You were in the car, knocking boots with that sweet little chippie who isn't your wife. Tammy, as I recall. Remember?"

Darcy swallowed heavily. His ruddy complexion had

gone a pale, pasty white. He flicked his muddy brown gaze toward Pansy, who appeared to be haggling with Martin over the price of one of Rivka's prints. Darcy's tongue flickered out from between his lips to lick them nervously.

"Don't tell Pansy," he whispered, almost pleading. "She'll kill me. Or divorce me, which would be worse. She'd take everything."

"I won't tell Pansy." Darcy recoiled from Tom's smile as though a snake had twisted itself across his face. "Not if you do exactly what I tell you."

"What did you have in mind?"

"Come with me. I just want you to make a few announcements."

Nobody recognized her, Lila realized as she passed within yards of Rivka without her sister noticing. A secret smile bloomed across Lila's face. Only Darren and Lance knew she had decided to come as Cleopatra. What fun she would have when Rivka discovered Lila's new look!

She debated about finding Tom first. No, she'd go greet her sister. If the evening went as Lila planned, once she spoke to Tom there would be no time to congratulate Rivka on the opening success of The Gallery on Second. She had better tell her now.

"Greetings, Your Highness." Lila lifted her chin up just as haughtily as her sister's.

Rivka stared at Lila for a long moment. "Lila-love?"

Lila burst into laughter. "I thought I could fool you. Guess not."

"It was your perfume." Rivka reached for Lila to give her a hug. Lila stepped forward, meeting a solid obstacle with her toe. From beneath Rivka's skirt, Mick let out a loud yelp.

"Sorry." Her fur-clad brother-in-law emerged from under Rivka's gown.

"What happened to Bo Peep?" Rivka asked. "Not that I'm complaining because you look fabulous!"

"Well, aren't we all just a bunch of queens." Darren joined them.

He looked gorgeous. His form-fitting red gown glittered with sequins. Lila checked his legs, just to be sure. Yes, he wore nude stockings.

They bussed each other's cheeks, careful not to smudge their carefully applied makeup. Darren then held her at arm's length to see her better. Lance nodded approvingly.

"Girl, you got it goin' on! When Mr. Gorgeous sees you. ..."

"He's here?" His parking space had been empty when she arrived.

"He went to check out the food." Darren leaned close to whisper to her. "Go find him, honey."

Lila took a deep breath and tried to quell her nervous excitement. "I will."

"You will what?" Rivka rapped poor Mick on the head with her fan again. He scowled, rubbed the sore spot, and ducked back beneath her gown.

"I'm going to find Tom." Lila waited for her sister's response.

Rivka only smiled. "I'm glad, Lila-love."

They hugged again, crushing Mick between them. He didn't complain, but bore it stoically. Lila bent down and kissed his cheek for his patience, then was off into the crowd.

She had just wiggled her way past a group of people

costumed as a cruise ship when the music stopped. The DJ, who had set up his portable dance floor and other equipment in one corner of the room, began asking everyone in the gallery for silence. Curious, Lila followed rest of the crowd as people began moving toward the small platform Rivka had planned to use to display sculptures. It was bare at the moment, making it the perfect place for someone to stand and make announcements.

Which was exactly what someone was doing. Two someone's in fact; one dressed as a rather rumpled Julius Caesar. Lila's stomach lurched. It was William Darcy. The other, the one who made her breath catch in her throat, was a handsome Mark Antony. Tom.

"Attention, everyone!" Tom had commandeered the DJ's microphone. The room quieted at his command, a massive feat since the place was jammed full. "My fellow Roman here has something to say."

Tom handed the mike to William, who took it between two fingers as though it were covered in slime. The man she had once thought moved the sun and stars didn't look well, Lila decided with mean satisfaction. Sweat had broken out on his brow, wilting his laurel leaves.

"Friends, Romans, countrymen," William began, and the crowd laughed appreciatively. "I have something to say."

William fell silent, casting a look of desperate disgust at Tom. Tom merely nodded stonily, directing William to the crowd. William cleared his throat.

"It has come to my attention that, by my words and actions, I have brought pain to a certain person here tonight."

The crowd murmured. Lila's heart jumped. Boldly, she began pushing her way to the front of the throng. She wanted to see this from up close.

"I just wanted to apologize." William sounded strained. Lila caught sight of a scowling Pansy and repressed a chuckle. William's wife looked ready to kill him. "Many of you tonight have had the pleasure of viewing the paintings in the gallery's Bold Room. As you may know, those paintings are all of Rivka Delaney's sister, Lila Lazin."

Lila had pushed her way to the front of the crowd. Behind her, a woman grumbled that she couldn't see over Lila's headpiece, but Lila didn't care. She didn't want to miss a word.

"I once told Lila Lazin that I thought she was not only unattractive, but of less than average intelligence as well." The mouth Lila had once found so handsome now pursed with anger. "I told her that by dating her, I was doing her a favor."

Some in the crowd gasped; others laughed. The laughter was different now, however. When William had begun speaking, they had been laughing with him. Now, as he obviously was aware, those who laughed, laughed at him.

"Jerk!" someone called from the back of the crowd, and this time more people burst into rude laughter.

"I wanted to say I was sorry." William was as stiff as any good soldier.

His fingers were white-knuckled on the microphone. Lila had never seen him so discomfited. The Iron Prince was falling off his pedestal, and she felt a little sorry for him.

William cleared his throat. "Lila Lazin is one of the most intelligent women I know. I broke up with her because she intimidated me. I wasn't man enough to handle her."

His last words came out in a strangled growl that sent shrieks of feedback bouncing from the speakers. His eyes spitting venom, William thrust the microphone back into

Tom's hand. Glaring at the crowd, the fallen Caesar prepared to get off the platform.

"William!" Lila's voice cut through the crowd like a knife through butter. She climbed the steps to stand between him and Tom. The crowd hushed.

"I always knew you were a snake, William." The microphone in Tom's hand sent her voice clear to the back of the room. "I didn't realize you were such an asp."

The silence that followed was broken by the sound of someone applauding. Lila looked to see Rivka, in all her queenly glory, clapping wildly from her corner. Rivka was joined by Mick, then Martin. Soon the room swelled with the sound of people clapping, applauding her and laughing at the crestfallen William, face the color of fresh strawberries. He stumbled off the platform, grabbed Pansy's hand, and disappeared into the crowd.

Lila turned to Tom as her heart thundered in her chest. He was smiling at her. She stepped into his embrace and didn't care that a roomful of people watched them. Feeling Tom's lips on hers was all that mattered.

"I'm sorry." She clung to him, mouth next to his ear. "I was stupid and afraid."

"It's all right." Tom held her shoulders. "I don't care. I'm sorry I didn't make you understand before how much I love you."

"And I love you. Nothing anybody says or does will ever change my mind."

"Kiss her!" someone yelled from the crowd.

"Antony and Cleopatra!" another voice called. "The perfect couple!"

She realized without embarrassment that the crowd had heard their every word. She didn't care. She would shout her love to the rooftops, if that was what it took. She loved Tom Caine, and he loved her.

All at once, Tom fumbled with something at his waistline. Confused, Lila watched as he pulled out a small velvet pouch. Dropping to his knees, Tom took her hand in one of his and the microphone in the other.

"Lila Lazin, I love you more than I ever thought I could love someone. You are the reason I wake up in the morning. Without you, I have nothing. Will you do me the honor of becoming my wife?"

The swarm of party goers was roaring, or perhaps it was only the blood pounding in her ears. Lila's knees trembled, and her fingers grew cold in Tom's hand. His hazel eyes shone at her, and his wonderful mouth smiled with such love she had to smile back.

There was only one right answer. "Yes."

As Tom slipped the diamond ring on her finger, the crowd's voice swelled as one, calling out congratulations and other well-wishes. Lila didn't hear them, though. All she heard was her own name breathed from the mouth of the man she loved.

"I love you, Lila." Then the shouts and cries of the other people in the room disappeared for her, because his was the only voice that would ever matter.

Author's Note:
Nothing In Common was originally published in 2002.

ALSO BY MEGAN HART

All the Lies We Tell

All the Secrets We Keep

A Heart Full of Stars

Always You

Broken

Castle in the Sand

Clearwater

Crossing the Line

Deeper

Dirty

Don't Deny Me

Everything Changes

Every Part of You

Flying

Hold Me Close

Indecent Experiment

Lovely Wild

Naked

Out of the Dark

Passion Model

Precious and Fragile Things

Reawakened Passions

Ride with the Devil

Selfish is the Heart

Stranger

Stumble into Love

Switch

Tear You Apart

Tempted

The Darkest Embrace

The Favor

The Resurrected: Compendium

The Space Between Us

Vanilla

ABOUT THE AUTHOR

I was born and then I lived awhile. Then I did some stuff and other things. Now, I mostly write books. Some of them use a lot of bad words, but most of the other words are okay.

I can't live without music, the internet, or the ocean, but I have kicked the Coke Zero habit. I can't stand the feeling of corduroy or velvet, and modern art leaves me cold. I write a little bit of everything from horror to romance, and I don't answer to the name "Meg."

Megan Hart is a USA Today, Publisher's Weekly and New York Times bestselling author who writes in many genres including mainstream fiction, erotic fiction, science fiction, romance, fantasy and horror. If you liked this book, please tell everyone you love to buy it. If you hated it, please tell everyone you hate to buy it.

Find me here!
www.meganhart.com
readinbed@gmail.com

Made in the USA
Monee, IL
14 September 2021